THE NOVELIZATION

Copyright © 2020 Disney Enterprises, Inc.
All rights reserved. Published by Disney Press, an imprint of Buena Vista Books, Inc. No part of this book may be reproduced or transmitted in any form or by any means, electronic or mechanical, including photocopying, recording, or by any information storage and retrieval system, without written permission from the publisher.
For information address Disney Press, 1200 Grand Central Avenue, Glendale, California 91201.

Printed in the United States of America
First Paperback Edition, June 2020
3 5 7 9 10 8 6 4 2
FAC-025438-20169

Library of Congress Control Number: 2019950924

ISBN 978-1-368-06122-3

For more Disney Press fun, visit www.disneybooks.com
Visit DisneyChannel.com and DisneyPlus.com

SUSTAINABLE
FORESTRY
INITIATIVE
Certified Chain of Custody
Promoting Sustainable Forestry
www.sfiprogram.org
SFI-01054
The SFI label applies to the text stock

THE NOVELIZATION

Adapted by Sarah Nathan

Based on *High School Musical*
The Musical: The Series, created by Tim Federle

Ðisnep PRESS
Los Angeles • New York

CHAPTER 01

THE AUDITIONS

Based on the episode

by Tim Federle

Miss Jenn pulled her car into the faculty parking lot of East High. It was the first day of school, and she was excited to start her new job as the drama teacher. She took a deep breath and looked down at her phone.

"Oh, come on!" she said, hitting the screen. The buffering interrupted the song "We're All in This Together" from her favorite High School Musical movie. She looked up from the screen to the East High banner hanging over the school's front doors. She had seen that red sign with white block letters so many times. And now here she was, ready to tackle the first day of school at the famous East High.

She got out of her car just as two boys on

skateboards whizzed by her. She was pressed against the car.

"Sorry!" one called out.

"Our bad!" the other said.

"All good!" Miss Jenn said with a smile. "No bad!"

As she turned to head into the school, she didn't realize her dress was caught in the car door.

Riiiiip.

"Great, first costume change," Miss Jenn muttered to herself. She shook off the mishap and joined the stream of students heading inside the school.

Walking ahead of Miss Jenn were Ricky Bowen and his best friend, Big Red.

"Today's the day, Big Red," Ricky said. He was holding his skateboard and helmet in his hands. "It's happening."

"Junior year, baby," Big Red said, grinning. "Might grow a mustache. Might do a lotta things."

"Dude," Ricky said, turning to look at his red-headed friend. "I'm talking about Nini. Today's the day we start over."

Inside the school, Nini Salazar-Roberts walked down the hallway with her best friend, Kourtney, sharing stories about her summer at drama camp. "Oh, wait, I want to show you a picture," Nini said, holding her phone up. "This was my costume in act two."

"Flawless," Kourtney said. "Love it."

"And this is the wig that almost fell off in the middle of my ballad," Nini continued.

Down the hall, Ricky and Big Red made their way into East High. "We texted. She sounded neutral," Ricky told Big Red as they walked. "Nothing about bad news or needing to have a big talk. Just 'Hey.' That's good, right?"

"Summers are no-man's-land, Ricky," said Big Red. "I don't know what 'Hey' means, and neither do you."

"I think it's good," Ricky said, trying to convince himself.

Nini and Kourtney continued their talk in front of Nini's locker. "And this . . ." Nini said.

Kourtney took the phone from Nini's hand. She

zoomed in on the hot guy in the photo. "Oh, I know who that is, Nini," she said, smiling.

"Girl, I'm like point two seconds away from making that my lock screen," Nini said with a twinkle in her eye. She turned to open her locker.

"I can't tell if you're glowing or you're sunburnt," Kourtney said.

Nini grinned. "Definitely glowing," she said. "I had the best summer ever."

"And what does . . . you-know-who have to say about all this?" Kourtney asked, leaning into her locker.

Nini took her phone back. "I'm waiting for the right time to tell him," she said.

"Yo! Nini!" Ricky said as he and Big Red approached the girls. "What's good?"

"How do you feel about right now?" Kourtney asked Nini.

"Hey," Ricky said.

"Hey," Nini replied. She took a deep breath. "Can

we talk?" She didn't wait for his response. "I met someone at camp," she said. "I didn't plan—"

Ricky slumped. It had been his idea to take a summer pause, but he hadn't thought that Nini would actually meet someone at drama camp. Sure, he had hung out with a couple of girls over the summer, but all he had done was talk about Nini the whole time.

"Wait, is this a joke?" he said, interrupting her.

"Still talking here," Nini said with great confidence.

"Oh, snap!" Kourtney exclaimed with pride.

"I didn't plan for it to happen. But it happened," Nini told him. "He was the music man. I was Marian the librarian. It's called a show-mance."

Big Red was trying to keep up with the conversation. "Wait, you went to librarian camp? That's a thing?"

"Please tell me you're joking," Ricky said, staring at Nini.

"I'm not," Nini told him. She turned to face him and looked him straight in the eye. "Come on, Ricky.

You know what you did. Or what you didn't do."

Unfortunately, Ricky knew exactly what she was talking about. There was no way either of them could forget that night in Nini's room when she had played the song for him. And how he had panicked and froze.

Under the twinkling lights strung across her room, the two had sat on Nini's bed watching skateboarding videos on Ricky's phone. Nini and Ricky had been dating for almost a year, and she was happy—really happy. Sophomore year at East High had been pretty great with Ricky by her side.

Ricky looked up at her. "Do my feet stink?" he asked. He lifted his foot off the bed. "I feel like my feet stink."

"No," Nini said. Then she smiled. "Sort of," she said, shrugging and leaning in for a quick kiss. "I think it's cute."

Ricky laughed. "And that is why we work!"

Nini's heart melted. "Check your Instagram," she said, excited to share an anniversary message she had posted for him.

Ricky sat up and looked at his feed. Nini's post appeared. It was a video of her playing the ukulele and singing a song she had written for him, mixed in with a montage of photos of the two of them over the past year. She wanted to tell Ricky that she loved him and the song was the perfect way. "I think I kinda, you know . . ." she sang sweetly.

Then, at the end of the video, Nini leaned closer to him.

"I do, Ricky," she said. "I love you."

Ricky stared at her. His brown eyes were wide.

And he was silent.

Now he was about to suffer the repercussions of that night.

"I . . . I don't believe this," Ricky said. He shook his head. "You're blowing me off for some theater punk you met four weeks ago? At a lake?"

"You kinda dumped me," Nini replied.

"It was a break! It wasn't a breakup," Ricky said.

"I'm sorry, Ricky, but it's a breakup now," she said.

"Hop off, girl," said Kourtney, clearly proud of her best friend.

"Stay out of it, Kourtney," said Big Red.

"You stay out of it," Kourtney replied. "I'm dismantling the patriarchy this year, and I'm not afraid to start with you."

Nini turned and walked away with Kourtney by her side.

"You crushed it," Kourtney whispered to her. "That could not have gone better."

Nini smiled to herself. She felt good. She was Nini 2.0, and junior year was off to a good start—a really good start.

The first day of a new school year at East High always began with a kickoff assembly. Principal Gutierrez stood at the podium at midcourt in the school gym. He introduced the new drama teacher, who happily took the microphone.

"My name is Miss Jenn," she told the students. "When I heard that the high school where *High School Musical* was shot had never staged a production of *High School Musical*, I was shocked as an actress, inspired as a director, and triggered as a millennial."

Nini was bouncing in her seat. "I've spent two years in the chorus at East High," she whispered. "Would it be insane to think I might actually have a shot at playing Gabriella?"

Kourtney gave her a hard look. "It would be insane for Nini 2.0 *not* to think that!"

"Auditions are tomorrow after school," Miss Jenn continued. "This show could change your lives. I'm saying this as a background dancer from the original movie. Third from the left, back row, red headband, and those are my real teeth."

Just then, a student ran over to Miss Jenn. She didn't release the microphone; instead, she introduced him as Carlos, the show's student choreographer. Carlos was the perfect person for the job. Not only was he the sophomore captain of the school color guard, but he was the official *High School Musical* historian at East High and had seen the movie at least thirty-seven times.

After the assembly, Mr. Mazzara, the school's science teacher, stopped in to Miss Jenn's new office. Startled, Miss Jenn spilled her coffee all over her blouse. She was going to need another costume change.

"Hey there," Mr. Mazzara said. "I know you're new here, but FYI, your assistant needs a hall pass if he's gonna be late for class."

"Oh, lord," Miss Jenn sighed as she mopped the coffee from her shirt. "Are hall passes still a thing? What is this, prison?"

Mr. Mazzara shook his head. "Uh, no," he said. "It's a professional learning environment."

"Sweetie, I'm the ultimate professional," she said.

"For instance," Mr. Mazzara said, scowling, "we don't call colleagues 'sweetie.'"

Carlos rushed into the office past Mr. Mazzara.

"Knock knock, Miss Jenn," he said. "I just want to report that the *High School Musical* hashtag I started is already trending."

"Well, of course it is," Miss Jenn said. "Your generation deserves to make its own mark on this classic. Watch out, world."

Later, in the cafeteria, Nini sat with Kourtney and E. J. Caswell, the handsome guy from her cell phone screen. It turned out the guy she met at drama camp also attended East High. "So, crazy idea," E.J. said to Nini. "What if we went in costume to the auditions?"

"Okay, I'm listening," Nini said coyly.

He showed her a photo on his phone of Gabriella wearing her iconic red dress from the movie. "For my leading lady, it is time to go full V. Hudge," E.J. said.

"Ooookay," Nini said, pushing the phone down. "Let's not get ahead of ourselves. Obviously, you're gonna get Troy, but I don't wanna jinx anything!"

Kourtney gave her a look. "That doesn't sound very Nini 2.0 to me!"

"We're a package deal, babe," E.J. said. "And all the talented senior girls graduated last year. This one is ours to lose."

Now a senior, E.J. had noticed Nini two years earlier when she'd played the back end of the cow in *Gypsy*. At drama camp, he'd seen her come out of her shell. Now she was ready to be his leading lady.

Nini looked at E.J. and smiled. "Literally, how did we never speak until this summer?"

Just as they kissed, E.J.'s friends from the water polo team came over to greet him.

Nini leaned over to Kourtney. "Is he the best or is he the best?" she gushed. Kourtney was happy for her friend, but she didn't want Nini's heart to be crushed again.

Across the cafeteria, Ricky sat with Big Red watching Nini.

"I can't believe this," Big Red said. "Nini is dating E.J. Caswell."

"Yes," Ricky said. "I have eyes."

"Co-captain of the water polo team, senior class treasurer," Big Red listed. "I mean, what are the odds the guy she hooks up with at camp goes to East High?"

"Apparently the odds are exceptionally good, Big Red," Ricky spat. He rose from the table and headed toward the cafeteria exit. Today was not going as Ricky had imagined. And worst of all, the one person he was used to going to for advice was currently on her honeymoon in the cafeteria.

After school, Nini visited her grandmother to tell her all about the new drama teacher and how excited—and nervous—she was about the upcoming school musical auditions. She confided that she had been having the same dream since she was a little girl: she was all alone on a big Broadway stage, and she opened her mouth to sing, but nothing came out.

"There's obviously something about being heard

that feels off-limits to you," her grandma said. "Do you not think you've earned it?"

"I don't know," Nini said. "How do you stop having a dream?"

"You live it," her grandma responded.

Over at Ricky's house, his dad, Mike, was struggling with the Instant Pot and a raw, cold chicken.

"Call Mom," Ricky told his dad. "It's like nine p.m. in Chicago. She can't still be in a meeting." When his dad didn't move, Ricky picked up his phone.

"She doesn't want to hear from me right now, okay?" Mike told his son. Ricky knew his parents were having a rough patch, but it still hurt to watch them struggle.

"This has nothing to do with you," Ricky's dad assured him, seeing the sadness in his son's eyes. "It's gonna be fine, bud."

Ricky didn't know much, but he knew his dad should be doing something. Didn't he want to fight to save his marriage? Suddenly, Ricky had an idea. He wasn't going to let Nini go without a fight. He would win her back by auditioning for the new musical. He went over to Big Red's to tell him about his plan.

"Do you even know the plot of *High School Musical*?" Big Red asked.

"Of course," Ricky said. "It's about Zac Efron dancing with a basketball."

Big Red shook his head. "Wrong!" he said. "It's about the character Troy having to choose between being true to his friend Chad or following his heart with Gabriella."

Ricky stared at Big Red. "Why do you know so much about *High School Musical*?"

"They play it on a loop at my allergist's office," he said. "You're out of your league. You can't pull this off."

Ricky took up the challenge. The next day, he borrowed a DVD of the film from the school library to study up before the auditions. Unfortunately, the DVD got stuck in the computer just as the end-of-the-day bell rang. Mr. Mazzara tried to help him get the DVD out, but the two struggled with the school computer. Zac Efron on repeat was Mr. Mazzara's worst nightmare. Ricky confessed to the flustered science teacher that he had been studying for the auditions.

"Stop wasting your time," Mr. Mazzara said. "You don't need to massage Miss Jenn's bruised ego just because her lights went out on Broadway."

Ricky finally gave up on getting the DVD out and headed for the door. He was going to be late to auditions—not a great way to start his high school theater career.

The auditorium was buzzing with excitement as the auditions were about to begin. Carlos clapped his hands to get everyone's attention.

E.J. stood with Nini, feeling very confident. Nini wasn't so sure of herself, especially after she saw Carlos's warm-up routine and the new girl who was killing the complicated dance number. Nini introduced herself and confessed she had never been cast as a lead before. "But this summer at drama camp, I went on for the lead when she got low-grade salmonella, so I'm ready," she said.

"I've never been to drama camp. Or been an understudy," the girl with the incredible high kicks said. "You'll have to tell me all about it." She put out her hand. "Gina. Sophomore. Transfer student."

Nini was a little surprised by how straightforward Gina was, but she shook her hand.

The students lined up on the stage, and Miss Jenn and Carlos moved down the row, assessing the possible cast and handing out audition packets.

Miss Jenn stopped in front of Ashlyn, E.J.'s cousin. "You," Miss Jenn said. "You're giving me uncommon depth. Ms. Darbus?"

Ashlyn beamed.

Miss Jenn looked at Ashlyn's application and smiled when she learned Ashlyn also played piano. "I always thought the drama teacher should have an act two power ballad. We'll sidebar."

Ashlyn was thrilled.

Next Miss Jenn marked Gina as a possible Gabriella. Gina pushed aside the audition packet. "I'm already off book," she told Carlos.

E.J. was next in the line. Miss Jenn took one look at the handsome senior and turned to Carlos. "Give him the Troy stuff. Who are we kidding?"

When Miss Jenn tried to hand Nini Kelsi's part, Nini took a deep breath. "Gabriella," she said, mustering up her courage. "I want to audition for Gabriella."

Carlos handed her the packet, and Nini grinned. She was going after what she wanted!

A wholesome-looking boy named Seb was next, and Miss Jenn asked if he would be reading for Ryan's part.

"I think he'd rather play Sharpay," Carlos told her.

"I love that," Miss Jenn said appreciatively. "That is so fresh."

E.J. was the first to audition. His good looks matched his smooth singing voice. Miss Jenn and

Carlos looked at each other approvingly. They were sold. Gina sang next, and her voice was just as amazing as her dance moves.

In the wings, Nini was freaking out. She turned to E.J. for some last-minute tips.

"Okay, you're doing the thing," he told her.

"What thing?" she asked.

"The thing where you talk in a vague British accent when you are nervous," he said. Luckily, he knew how to talk her down—and out of the accent.

"You're a total weirdo," he joked. "And one hundred percent real. And that's why I love you."

His words sank in, and Nini thought back to the night when she'd said those same words to Ricky. She shook off the memory and went out onstage. Just as Nini was about to start her audition, Ricky burst through the auditorium door.

"Am I too late?" he called.

"We're all set on Troys," Miss Jenn said. "We're low on Chads. You can read after the Gabriellas."

"But I only studied the Troy scenes in the movie!" Ricky said.

"Troy would have arrived on time," Carlos told him.

E.J. gave a loud cheer of encouragement for Nini, which startled Miss Jenn and made her spill her coffee on the lighting board in front of her. The stage lights went dark. "Nini, let's wait till the lights go back on. I don't want this to throw you." Miss Jenn said. "I'm not thrown," Nini said. And she began to sing "Start of Something New" a cappella. Ricky held up his phone flashlight to shine it on Nini, and E.J. leapt up to do the same. Caught between them, Nini stayed focused and imagined herself as Gabriella, red dress and all.

Miss Jenn was impressed. She made some notes just as the theater lights came back on.

"You, late boy—let's do the Chad sides," she told Ricky.

Ricky took the Chad pages and read two sentences, then crumpled the paper up. He ad-libbed his own lines. "Maybe it's the way Gabriella always had your back. And maybe you can't stop beating yourself up for totally blowing it with her."

Miss Jenn looked down at her script. "Was this in the movie?" she whispered to Carlos.

Ricky went on, looking at Nini. "And look, Troy, even if you never said the L-word to Gabriella, because that's not a word your parents even say to each other anymore, maybe it doesn't mean you don't. Maybe it just means you were waiting for the right time to say it."

E.J. put his arm around Nini. Ricky loved *his* girl?

Just when Nini thought things couldn't get more awkward, Ricky reached for his guitar and played her song, "I Think I Kinda, You Know."

Miss Jenn was wowed. "I think that's all we need today," she said.

Ricky left the stage and Nini ran after him. She caught up with him in the hallway.

"What are you doing here?" Nini asked. "You hate musicals."

"That is harsh," Ricky said. "The new me thinks musicals are . . . awesome."

Nini narrowed her eyes. "Well, let me tell you about the old me," she said. "The old me had her heart broken, and then she went away and found herself. And you don't get to show up now just to try and . . . confuse things!"

"You think that is why I'm here? No, I always believed in you," Ricky said. "In us. Even if I sucked at showing it. That's why I'm here."

Carlos pushed past Nini and Ricky waving a sheet of paper. "Clear!" he yelled, followed by all the students who had just auditioned.

"I . . . don't *not* love you," Ricky said under his breath.

Carlos tacked the cast list up. Miss Jenn had "instincts" and wanted to post the cast right away.

Nini and Kourtney saw the list first. Nini was Gabriella! Gina won the part of Taylor, and would be Nini's understudy.

E.J. backed away from the list. "She thinks I'm a Chad?"

"Holy crap, dude," Big Red said as he saw the list. Ricky lifted his eyes. His name was first on the list . . . in the part of Troy Bolton.

CHAPTER 02

THE READ-THROUGH

Based on the episode
by Oliver Goldstick

The first *High School Musical* read-through was in the basement of East High. Carlos had set desks in a circle with cast name cards on each. E.J. noted right away that he was not sitting next to Nini and was about to switch the seating assignment, but he caught Ashlyn's eye and left the cards alone.

Kourtney, who had joined the costume crew, looked at Ricky and Big Red across the room. "How are you going to get through seventy-four rehearsals with him?" she whispered to Nini.

"I won't make eye contact," Nini replied. She'd waited a long time to be the lead at East High. She wasn't going to let Ricky ruin this for her.

Miss Jenn was about to begin the read-through when Carlos told her the stage manager, Natalie Bagley, wasn't coming. Miss Jenn looked around until her eyes landed on Big Red. "Yoo-hoo, ginger boy, can you read?"

Big Red mumbled, "Um . . . not really."

Miss Jenn handed him a script. "Well, you're reading now. Just the stage directions." She sat down at her assigned desk and smiled at her cast. "I realize that you all walked in here as strangers, but after today, you're a family," she said. "Please take your neighbors' hands. Feel each other's energy. Let the silence speak volumes. In a world full of no, this is a space full of yes!"

Nini took Gina's hand and then looked down at Ricky's hand in hers. Her nose twitched when she smelled his cologne. Did he think spraying a whole bottle of cologne would cover up what he had done and win her over? She pulled her hand away.

E.J. rolled his eyes as Big Red haltingly read the stage directions. At the rate they were going, act one could last all month. Everyone was relieved when it was time to take a break.

"I was hoping we'd get to sing the songs," E.J. said to Nini.

"I guess Miss Jenn wants us to really pay attention to the lyrics," she replied.

"Yeah, but she can't sing them like you can." He leaned down to kiss his girlfriend.

Nini smiled at the sweet gesture, but the kiss was interrupted by her phone vibrating. She quickly glanced at her phone and giggled.

E.J. noticed. "Who's that from?"

"What?" Nini asked, tucking her phone away. "Oh, it's nothing."

E.J. looked over at Ricky, who was staring at his phone. He narrowed his eyes.

Across the room, Miss Jenn whispered to Carlos. "What happened to our Troy and Gabriella? Where are the sparks from the audition?"

"Should we think about recasting?" Carlos responded.

"Absolutely not," Miss Jenn told him. "My instincts are impeccable. I'm not scared of a challenge."

Miss Jenn came up with a plan to warm up Nini and Ricky. She called an early-morning rehearsal for just the two of them. "We're diving into page ninety-seven," she told them when they arrived at the auditorium.

"You wanna rehearse this?" Nini asked, flipping to the back of her script. "It's not even a scene. Just one line."

"Then there's the kiss," Miss Jenn said.

"Um, I don't remember a kiss," Nini said.

Miss Jenn smiled. "It was very much there in the original film. The kiss ended up on the cutting room floor. A little racy for its time."

Nini was flustered.

Later in the day, Miss Jenn called Nini to her office. "Sweetie," she said, "I added the kiss because our production needs it. I've also added a cowbell, a power ballad for the drama teacher, and a Wildcat cheer for the curtain call."

Nini listened. She didn't want to get into the whole Ricky history with Miss Jenn. "It's complicated," she said. "I just can't kiss Ricky right now. I have a new boyfriend. He's playing Chad."

Miss Jenn leaned across her desk. "Nini, trust the process. Your character only has eyes for Troy."

Nini didn't know that E.J. was standing outside Miss Jenn's door. He was fuming. What hold did Ricky have over this new drama teacher? He'd gotten the lead, and now Miss Jenn had written in a kissing scene? He found Ashlyn at her locker and vented his frustration. He also voiced his concerns about Ricky trying to win back Nini. Ashlyn told him he was paranoid.

"Really?" E.J. huffed. "Why did Ricky text Nini at the read-through? And why wouldn't she tell me who it was?"

"She doesn't have to tell you," Ashlyn said. "Dating her doesn't mean you own her."

E.J. shifted his feet. "I need you to borrow her phone for me," he said.

"As in steal?" Ashlyn said, closing her locker. "You've just gone up three levels of scary. If she ever found out, she would never forgive you. Or me. You want to take that risk?"

"Ashlyn, please," E.J. said with a sigh. "She's not like the other girls I've dated. Nini's real. She makes me better."

At rehearsal after school, Carlos was teaching the cast the curtain call number. This made no sense to Nini and Ricky, since they hadn't even gotten through the first scene. Carlos explained that according to *The Big Book of Broadway*, you start with the dance that takes the longest to learn.

"Okay, people!" Carlos yelled. "Let's take it from three counts of eight before Troy and Gabriella's entrance for the bows."

Ricky was in way over his head. He tried to do the

steps, but he really was not a dancer. He started to have a little fun with the off-rhythm moves. Nini was not amused.

"What was he doing?" Nini asked Carlos.

Ricky looked at Nini. "Why are you talking to him? I'm right here."

"Because you're not here," Nini said. "At least not for the right reasons."

The whole cast stopped to listened in on their conversation.

"Ricky," Nini began, "you hate musicals. You only did this so we'd be in each other's grills."

Carlos clapped his hands. "Back to the dance!" he commanded.

Nini couldn't stop. "Now you are wearing some weird cologne on your neck and wasting everyone's time by making fun of something that the rest of us take seriously."

Ricky looked hurt. "I take this seriously."

"No, you don't," Nini replied. "You don't take anything seriously. You coast. And the second someone asks you to make a commitment, you make a joke or sink into some imaginary hole in the floor."

"I didn't sink, Nini. I just wasn't ready to say it then. But I went to that audition to show you—"

Nini interrupted him. "Only because I'd met someone else. You wanted to drag me back into tenth grade like my summer never happened. But if you really cared about me, you'd let someone who wants to play this part play it."

Ricky nodded. "Like E.J.?"

Carlos stepped between them. "Can we at least try the dip?" he begged.

Ricky pushed past Carlos and passed Miss Jenn as she walked in. "Where are you going, Troy?" she asked.

"It's Ricky," he said as the door slammed behind him.

Big Red followed Ricky into the hallway and out of the school.

"Operation Troy was a huge mistake," Ricky told his friend. "I've made things worse."

Carlos flew through the school doors. "There you are!" he said to Ricky. "Miss Jenn wants everyone back in the room."

Ricky kept walking. "Tell Miss Jenn I am done," he said. "Sorry I can't dance like Fred Rogers."

"It's Fred Astaire," Carlos said. "Fred Rogers is Mr. Rogers. . . ."

"Save it, Carlos," Ricky said. "You don't want me in this. If I go back, Nini will probably quit. And you need her a lot more than you need me."

Ricky just needed some alone time to think about Nini, the musical, and what was going on at home. He took off on his skateboard.

Gina had been watching the drama from a nearby bench. She realized if Ricky stayed in the show, that there was a good chance Nini would drop out and she could take over the lead. She followed Ricky to the skate park.

"Hey, you," Gina said, greeting Ricky.

"Gina, what are you doing here?" Ricky asked.

"Babysitting. My neighbor asked me to watch her

kid," she said. "So is it true? You dropped out?"

"I haven't made it official yet," he said, shrugging. "But yeah, I guess so."

Gina shook her head. "That sucks," she said. "Having you there gave us all street cred. I mean, you're not a drama geek. You've never sung a song outside of your shower."

"Did Miss Jenn send you?" Ricky asked.

"Please," Gina said, laughing. "I think I scare her."

Ricky laughed. "You are a little scary."

"I'm a transfer student. You either eat or get eaten," she told him. She watched his face. "That's why I was stoked when she cast you. Outsiders keep everyone else on their toes. You kept us real. Look, you don't need Carlos to tell you how to move. You have your own style."

Ricky wasn't sure what to make of this conversation. He went off to skate as Gina put her earphones back on and sat back listening to "Breaking Free." Ricky felt free on his skateboard, too. The skate park was a great place to clear his head and think about his next move. He decided that if he stayed up all night practicing the steps to prove to Nini that he was serious about the show, she might realize that he wasn't willing to quit on them.

During fifth period the next day, Nini spotted Ricky and Carlos in the back corner of the library. Hiding in the stacks, she saw Ricky doing the dance number for Carlos—perfectly. She left before they saw her. Ricky's efforts surprised her and made her think twice about what she was feeling toward him. She ducked into the auditorium to avoid E.J. coming down the hall. Inside, she found Ashlyn sitting at the piano singing.

"Miss Jenn asked me to compose a song for my character," Ashlyn said. "I'm playing Ms. Darbus."

"I know who you're playing," Nini said, smiling.

"We don't have to talk about E.J.," Ashlyn said, feeling uncomfortable. "Do you want to talk about E.J.?"

Nini's phone was buzzing. "Oh, this has to stop," she said, looking at the screen.

"It doesn't matter who texted you," Ashlyn said, thinking of E.J. "It's no one's business."

"One of my moms has been texting me fortune cookie messages to keep me balanced," Nini told her.

Ashlyn tried to get out of the awkward silence by playing a few chords on the piano. Nini joined her in the soulful song "Wondering." It was all about regrets. While the two girls got lost in the song, Ricky walked in. Nini wondered how much of the song he had heard.

"Miss Jenn wants everyone downstairs," he told them.

Nini stared at Ricky for a minute, then quickly grabbed her things and joined the cast. Miss Jenn was showing off her *High School Musical* memorabilia—Gabriella's phone from the movie. Everyone oohed and aahed at the phone.

E.J. looked down at his bag and saw Nini's phone. He looked over at Ashlyn and mouthed, *Thank you.*

"You're welcome," Gina said, coming up behind him. "We want the same thing, hon, but it's gonna take a little teamwork."

E.J. watched Gina strut off and wondered exactly what she meant.

"Places for the top of the ski lodge!" Miss Jenn called.

E.J. zipped up his bag with Nini's phone and slung the backpack over his shoulder.

THE WONDERSTUDIES

Based on the episode
by Zach Dodes

Ashlyn left rehearsal and found E.J. waiting for her in his car. He looked upset about something.

"She told him she loved him," he told Ashlyn.

"Who?" she asked.

"Nini. I found an archived post on her Instagram," E.J. told her as he looked down at Nini's phone.

Ashlyn took a deep breath. "E.J., you can't just go snooping around someone's phone like a creepy stalker."

"I play to win, Ash," E.J. said. "Have we met?"

E.J. showed her Nini's anniversary song video.

"Whatever, that was four months ago," Ashlyn said. "They are over. Ancient history. There is no Ricky."

Just then, Nini's phone rang, and Ricky's face

appeared on the screen. Ashlyn moved the phone away from E.J. "Don't answer it!"

The call went to voice mail.

"You need to return this," Ashlyn said. "And do not listen to that voice mail."

E.J. lowered his head. "I will . . . I mean . . . I won't," he said.

Ashlyn stared at him. "You're gonna listen to it, aren't you?" She shook her head with disdain and got out of the car. "Forget the ride. I'll walk home," she said.

E.J. couldn't stop himself. He listened to the message from Ricky, who poured his heart out to Nini. Hearing the song Nini and Ashlyn sang, he wondered what Nini was thinking when she sang those lyrics. "You can just ignore this whole message and we can pretend it never happened," Ricky said. "Okay? Poof. Gone."

And with one tap, that is what E.J. did to Ricky's message. Deleted. Poof. Gone.

Nini had spent the evening looking for her phone. The next morning, she rushed into rehearsal, where the cast was in the middle of "Stick to the Status Quo."

"Nini," Miss Jenn said. "Where were you? We've been here for an hour."

"I'm sorry," Nini said. "I lost my phone, and I finally picked it up at Lost and Found. . . ." She stopped and looked around. "Wait, did you say an hour?"

Miss Jenn moved closer to her. "Gina sent you and me a text asking if we could come in early so she could talk through a new idea. You didn't get it?"

Nini shook her head. "Um, no, because my phone was missing."

"Well, honey," Miss Jenn said, "you've gotta keep better track of your stuff. A real triple threat means singing, acting, and being organized." Miss Jenn smiled at Gina. "Gina pitched a new dance break for Gabriella and Taylor in the middle of 'Stick to the

Status Quo.' She got Carlos to work it all out with her, and it's dazzling!"

Gina held up two bedazzled lunch trays.

Nini glared at Gina. Was it possible that Gina had stolen her phone? Gina scheduled an early-morning rehearsal that she knew Nini would miss, and then choreographed a new dance number she knew Nini couldn't do. If Gina was willing to steal the spotlight, what else was she willing to steal?

"Gina really wants my part in the show and she's basically willing to kill me to get it," Nini confided in Kourtney later when the girls were at Nini's house.

"I could have told you that days ago," Kourtney said. She paused. "Wait, hang on, I did."

"But now she's stealing phones and inventing special new ways for me to hurt myself," Nini said. She took out her iPad. "So here's a list of possible solutions I came up with." She showed the screen to Kourtney with a list of six items:

1) TALK TO MISS JENN

2) MAGICALLY LEARN THE DANCE

3) HAVE MY MOMS YELL AT HER MOM

4) QUIT THE SHOW

5) EAT SO MUCH ICE CREAM

6) STEAL SOMETHING BACK

Kourtney considered the list. "Okay," she said. "We can scratch off number six, because that is an act of war."

Nini shrugged and pulled out Gina's dance shoes from her backpack. "Too late," she said. "I thought you'd veto the ice cream."

In Big Red's basement, Ricky was regretting leaving the phone message for Nini. He hadn't heard from her, so it seemed like it might have been the wrong move.

"You broke her heart," Big Red said. "You crashed her play, bugged her for a while, and then you left an extra-sad voice mail."

"You think maybe it's time to move on?" Ricky asked.

"I mean, I wouldn't, but you have that other thing," Big Red told him. "Pride." He smiled at Ricky. "Be yourself. Be the bigger man. It's like that scene in the movie where Troy tells his teammates, 'You're my guys and this is our spam.'"

Ricky did a double take. "Spam? When does he say that?"

Big Red shrugged. "I just realized that my allergist keeps the sound off in the waiting room and maybe I can't read lips."

At school the next day, Nini pulled E.J. to the back corner of the school library and showed him what she'd done.

"You stole Gina's shoes?" he asked. "What if she retaliates?"

"Then I'll come back at her twice as hard," Nini said. "I will rain down hellfire, you understand?"

"Nini," E.J. said, "I gotta be honest. This doesn't feel like you."

"It didn't feel like me," Nini confessed. "But I stepped into the light. I play to win now." She looked up at him. "I thought you'd be proud."

"But stealing?" E.J. asked. "You're better than that."

Nini cracked. "Ugh, maybe you're right. I do like that you see me that way. You're a good person, E.J. I don't know if it's because you're a senior or because someone raised you right . . . but I wish I had whatever you've got inside you. It's like confidence mixed with morals." She leaned toward him. "And about a dozen abs. Thanks for being you."

She gave him a kiss and walked away, and E.J.'s guilt felt like a thousand pounds weighing on him. If only she knew what he had done and how insecure he really felt. He walked out of the library and found Ashlyn sitting in the stairwell. She was surprised to see E.J. feeling so guilty. "I'm not the person I want to be," he said. "I am not the person Nini thinks I am." He looked at his cousin. "What should I do?"

Ashlyn had one simple thought. "Apologize," she told him.

E.J. had bigger ideas. He wanted to write an apology song. He knew Ashlyn wrote songs, so he asked if she would help him. She relented and said she would send him something she had been working on, but she didn't think E.J. would be able to charm himself out of this situation.

Mr. Mazzara looked both ways down the empty school hallway. When he was sure no one was there, he ducked into a storage closet and switched on the light. He had doubts about Miss Jenn's teaching credentials and her story about being in *High School Musical.* He'd lost four members of his robotics club to the cast, and he needed those students for funding if the club was going to go to China for a conference. He reached up for one of the many boxes of *High School Musical* memorabilia stored there and pulled down an old movie poster. Squinting, he took a photo with his phone to enlarge the picture.

"Aha!" he exclaimed. There was Miss Jenn! She wasn't a featured dancer. She was merely an extra, one of many in the background.

"Did you return Gina's shoes?" Kourtney asked Nini later that night when the girls were hanging out in Nini's room.

Nini had planned on returning the shoes, but then she'd overheard a conversation between Gina and a costume designer that made her fume.

"You might want to put Gabriella in a color that pops a little more," Gina had told the costume designer. "She's already kinda bland. Not as a person—sweetest girl in the world—but as an actress. I just don't want her to get lost in the crowd."

After Nini heard that comment, she took Gina's water bottle.

"Look, you don't have to say it—" Nini began.

Kourtney put her bag on the bed. "I know. I stole three scarves, some jewelry, and her laptop," Kourtney confessed. "Yeah, we are going to jail!"

E.J.'s song wasn't coming along so well. He went over to Ashlyn's for help. As she sat in the kitchen listening and trying not to laugh, E.J. sang his attempt at an apology song. He knew it wasn't the best . . . or enough.

"There's a lot to admire," Ashlyn said as he wrapped up his mini performance.

E.J. cringed. He knew what he had to do. "Tomorrow I will tell her what happened and straight up apologize," he said.

Ashlyn nodded and hoped E.J. would follow through. "She might forgive you," she said.

"Would you?" E.J. asked.

"I'm proud of you either way," Ashlyn told her cousin.

Ricky and E.J. faced each other in the rehearsal room. They were both resigned to playing their parts and getting the scene done. Miss Jenn directed them to take it from the top. "Remember, these two boys are best bros," she told them. "Which is a sacred thing, for reasons I'll never understand."

The lines between Troy and Chad were forced and empty, and not one person in the rehearsal believed a word either boy said.

Miss Jenn clapped her hands. "Okay!" she said. "Let's loosen up, pass some energy back and forth. Let's use the ball and improvise!"

E.J. wasn't sure what she wanted. "Just say whatever?" he asked.

"Chad it up!" Miss Jenn said.

"Troy," E.J. said to Ricky, "you're the best player we've got. We're so dang lucky." He passed the ball with a heavy throw.

Ricky caught the ball and whizzed it right back to E.J. "I wouldn't be anything without you," he said.

The ball was getting faster with each throw.

"You deserve everything that's coming your way," E.J. said.

"Back atcha, dude," Ricky replied as he heaved the ball.

The ball smacked between them a few more times. "Back at you infinity plus one!" Ricky said. And this time the ball slammed E.J. in the face. Now E.J.'s lip was bleeding.

"Okay," Miss Jenn said, moving in. "Let's take a soft ten. E.J., honey, let's get you some ice."

Ricky followed E.J. into the bathroom. E.J. wanted nothing to do with him. "Do me a favor and stay away from me and Nini, okay?"

"I'm just trying to say I'm sorry," Ricky said.

E.J. narrowed his eyes. "You want to apologize? You can start with that thirsty voice mail you left for Nini last night. She doesn't need to hear from you anymore."

Ricky felt like E.J. had hurtled another basketball at him. He thought Nini would have respected a private voice mail. Had she played E.J. that message?

Back in the rehearsal room, Mr. Mazzara walked in and asked to speak to Miss Jenn in the hallway. He was ready to call her out on her exaggerated *High School Musical* claim.

"It was my understanding that a big reason you got this job was because of your experience as a featured dancer in the film." He showed her the blurry photo on his phone. "That's you in 2006," he said. "With all the other extras who didn't dance or sing or even have a real name."

Carlos appeared with coffees and could sense the tension. "Miss Jenn, is he bothering you?" he asked.

Mr. Mazzara was not amused. "You ought to spend a little less time worrying about your drama teacher and a little more time trying to make some friends under the age of thirty-five," the science teacher snapped.

Miss Jenn told Carlos everything was fine and

asked him to warm up the cast with "Stick to the Status Quo."

"Don't ever talk to one of my students like that again," Miss Jenn scolded.

"Your students," Mr. Mazzara spat. "Do you even have a teaching credential?"

Miss Jenn was firm. "I may have fudged a thing two on my résumé, but I'm here because I believe in these kids. Not because they are going to be Broadway stars, but because they aren't. They're weird and unusual and quirky. They come here at the end of the day, and everything they get made fun of for outside that room is what makes them shine inside it. You may think Carlos has no friends, but the moment I posted that cast list, he got seventeen new ones."

She opened the door, revealing the cast singing and having a great time. There was nothing Mr. Mazzara could say. It was theater magic.

At the end of the song, Nini returned Gina's things. "We have to find a way to respect each other, and I know that starts with me," she told her. "So when I thought you took my phone, I may have gone a little crazy. The point is, I've come into possession of a few of your things, and I'd like to return them to you. I'm not going to be a doormat for you . . . and I'm also not going to be a klepto."

Before Nini left, Gina called her back. "Just one thing, before you go. I didn't have your phone last night."

Nini felt dizzy. As she walked outside of East High, Ricky ran up to her. "I know we're not a couple anymore, but I thought there was a little trust left between us," he said.

"I can't do this now," Nini said, trying to move away.

"Fine," Ricky said. "But the next time I bare my soul in a voice mail, keep it to yourself. I don't need to hear from E.J. that it was wrong and stupid."

Nini turned to Ricky. "Wait, what voice mail?"

She spied E.J. at the curb with a bunch of his

water polo friends. "You heard this from E.J.?" she asked. She looked at Ricky's hurt face and then over at E.J., who gave her a wave. E.J. had her phone last night! This was a plot twist she didn't expect.

BLOCKING

Based on the episode
by Margee Magee

Nini rushed down the school stairs to get to rehearsal. She had been avoiding E.J. all day. From the top of the stairwell, E.J. called her name and hurried to catch up with her. She ignored him and continued to descend.

Finally, E.J. was at her side. They usually sat together at lunch, and Nini had been nowhere to be found. When he asked where she had been, Nini stopped walking and turned to confront him. "Fine. Want to know where I was at lunch? I was in the computer lab bribing some hacker to crack into my phone and recover a message you deleted when you stole it!"

The entire cast was standing outside the doors—and listening to their conversation.

"Nini, why do you think—" E.J. started.

Nini stopped him. "Please. Gina's not the wonder-study I need to worry about." She was in no mood for E.J. to try to charm his way out of this.

"I was spiraling," E.J. confessed. "I told you I loved you, and you couldn't even say it back. You said it to Ricky, and I see the way Ricky looks at you. I know you guys have a lot more history. . . ."

"He would never steal my phone," she said, glaring at E.J. "Don't make this about Ricky."

"That is what this is about," E.J. tried to explain. "I am trying to hold on to what we had over the summer."

Nini stared into E.J.'s eyes. "I was, too," she whispered. "But you know what? Summer is over." She looked over and noticed the cast hanging on their every word.

"Is the door locked?" Nini asked. "Why can't we get in?"

"Natalie Bagley's emotional-support hamster is missing," Ashlyn explained. "He got loose. Carlos and Gina are trying to help her find her. Him. It."

A shrill scream came from behind the rehearsal room doors.

"Think they found it," Ashlyn said.

Ricky's living room was a mess of old Chinese-food boxes and dirty socks, making his search for scene seven from his script impossible. His dad was trying to straighten the house up. Ricky's mom was coming in from Chicago today, and the plan was for the family to meet for dinner at a restaurant after rehearsal. He was feeling stressed by the impending reunion, so he grabbed his skateboard and backpack. He'd borrow someone else's script at rehearsal.

The front door opened, and Ricky's mom came in with her luggage. She'd caught an earlier flight and was thrilled to see her son.

"I've missed you," she gushed, giving Ricky a big hug. She looked around the messy living room, a little shocked.

Ricky's dad was clearly uncomfortable. "We agreed we would do this at the restaurant."

"Agreed to do what?" Ricky asked, looking from one parent to the other. "Can we do whatever we're doing at dinner now?" When his parents avoided his question, Ricky turned to his mom. "Talk to me, guys. Are we moving to Chicago?"

"No, I am," his mom said. "Sweetheart, we've decided to legally separate."

Ricky had thought his mom was back to work things out. He felt the sting of her words.

"This is not your fault, Ricky," his mom said. "You've actually been the one thing that's held your dad and I together these past few years."

The room started to spin. Ricky couldn't listen to this. "I've got rehearsal. I'm not sure when I get out. It's a musical, lots of scenes. It could be tomorrow."

He bolted out the door and headed to school.

E.J. took Nini's hand as their discussion continued. "Sometimes a relationship needs one person looking out for the other," he said. "It wasn't divine intervention that got you into Marian the librarian's costume."

Nini took a moment to understand what E.J. had said. "You were responsible for making Emily Pratt spend opening night with her head in the toilet?" She searched his eyes. "Did you poison her so I could go on?"

"Take it down a notch," E.J. said, laughing uncomfortably. "I slipped her a bad deviled egg." He saw Nini's reaction. "What? You got the lead! Was that gonna happen if I hadn't stepped in?"

Carlos came out of the rehearsal room. They had not found the hamster. Carlos had screamed when Natalie stepped on his foot, but he'd recovered and was calling rehearsal to order. "Miss Jenn just talked to Ricky. He's running late," he said.

"Who cares?" E.J. mumbled.

"You might, considering you're his understudy," Carlos said. "We're blocking the Troy-Gabriella duet." He looked over at E.J. and Nini. "You're on, lovers."

As rehearsals began, Nini and E.J. stood on opposite ends of the stage. The tension between the two was palpable.

"Can I get you to move a little closer to each other?" Miss Jenn asked. "Come on, guys. We are blocking this as a love story, not a SARS epidemic."

Seb played the opening chords of "What I've Been Looking For," and Nini and E.J. started to sing, but the song was more like a battle song than a duet.

Miss Jenn put her hands up. "Okay, freeze," she said. "Nini, this reprise comes at a decisive moment in the story, once your hearts have joined. It's a love song."

Nini looked over at Miss Jenn. "Were you not getting that?" she asked innocently.

"I'd like you to get to his heart without cracking his rib cage," Miss Jenn explained.

Ricky burst into the room. "Sorry I'm late," he said, seeming slightly frazzled.

When Ricky didn't have his scene seven or a pencil, Miss Jenn scolded him and the cast. "When you come to rehearsal, people, you must come prepared," she said, sounding frustrated. "Come back when you are punctual, park your distractions at the door, and take the work inside here seriously." She ended rehearsal and asked Ricky to meet her in her office.

In Miss Jenn's office, Ricky confessed his parents were splitting up. Miss Jenn's parents had divorced when she was in high school, and Ricky's story struck a chord with her. While she was talking, Ricky spotted Natalie's hamster eating Miss Jenn's power bar on her desk. The hamster got away, and Ricky tried to get Miss Jenn to agree to let him stay overnight in her office.

Miss Jenn looked at Ricky with concern. "You can't stay here. You should go home and be with your family."

Ricky left her office, feeling there was no place he would rather *not* be than home.

E.J. was at his locker when Gina appeared behind him.

"Now you have a chance to be a hero," Gina said.

"Stay away from me," E.J. said.

"Girls like Nini love a comeback," Gina continued.

"You set me up, then sold me out. So if I were you, I'd cool it."

Gina didn't flinch. "Oh, please don't waste energy hating on me. Start thinking of the long game." She smiled sweetly. "Opening night is six weeks out, dude. Follow me, you'll have the part of Troy and the girl."

"Hate to tell you this," E.J. said, switching out some books from his locker, "but around here, seniors don't follow sophomores." He grabbed his backpack and walked away.

Gina leaned back on the locker. She had moved so many times and was used to reinventing herself. She knew if she acted like a confident theater veteran, people wouldn't catch on that it was fake . . . for a little while. Above the water fountain across the hall, she spotted a poster for the homecoming dance at East High. Suddenly, a plan formed in her mind. E.J. was going to take her.

Since rehearsal was cancelled, Nini and Kourtney headed to the coffeehouse in town. Nini spotted a cute couple at a nearby table and glared at them.

"Who steals a person's phone?" she asked Kourtney. She felt like she didn't know her own boyfriend and was crushed. She'd once looked like half of that cute couple, but now the charade was over.

"It's called a blind spot," Kourtney told her. Kourtney wondered why Nini seemed like she was on the warpath. She asked her bestie if she'd eaten anything today.

Kourtney checked her phone before she got up to get the two of them some food. There was a text from Tonya Freeman, a senior on the costume crew. She had vetoed all of Kourtney's suggestions. "She treats me like a child," she muttered.

"Have you told Miss Jenn?" Nini asked.

"I don't need Miss Jenn to fight my battles," Kourtney said. She went up to the counter, leaving Nini to watch the couple. She couldn't help but think back to a time during camp when E.J. had been so sweet. She had really trusted him.

"Hey, don't look now, but your shark's cousin is here," Kourtney said when she returned.

Ashlyn caught Nini's eye and turned around to exit the coffeehouse.

Nini ran out the door to follow her. "Ashlyn, you don't have to avoid me," she said, catching up to her.

Ashlyn unlocked her bike and started to head out.

"No matter what happens between me and E.J., there's no bad blood between us," Nini said. "I mean, you might have some because you're related to him, but that's not your fault."

Ashlyn didn't want to be in the middle. Nini quickly surmised that Ashlyn knew all about E.J.'s summer scheming.

"E.J., he tends to do the wrong things for the right reasons," Ashlyn said.

"You can't possible defend him," Nini said.

"I'm not," Ashlyn said. "I know what he did sucks, but he loves you and he's hurting right now and—"

"And what?" Nini asked. "What am I supposed to do?"

"Find some way to forgive him?" she asked.

Nini wasn't sure she could do that.

Big Red blew up an air mattress in his bedroom for Ricky. He was trying to distract Ricky with a funny story about a girl he had seen on YouTube eating dog kibble, but nothing was helping. Ricky's parents were splitting up and he was upset. He didn't want to deal . . . or go home. But Ricky couldn't fall asleep. Between Big Red's labored breathing and the strange noises coming from his sleep sound machine, Ricky couldn't fall asleep. He tossed and turned and finally picked himself up and left.

He wound up at Nini's house, talking to one of her moms. Carol was always there for him, and he really appreciated the way she sprang into action. She talked to his dad and explained Ricky was going to sleep over and then she set him up in the living room. She just didn't clear all that with Nini.

Nini heard voices downstairs and went to see what was going on. She saw the couch made up for an overnight guest. Carol told her that Ricky was going to stay the night. Nini tried to protest, but Carol stopped her short. She explained that Ricky's mom was back, but that she wasn't going to be staying long. And that no matter how bad Nini's day had been, Ricky's day had probably been a lot worse.

Ricky felt a little silly coming down the stairs in Carol's T-shirt and pajama pants.

"I probably should have called you and asked how you felt about me being here," he told Nini. She could tell he really needed to talk, and Nini knew she was the one person he could really open up to. He had to . . . he was bursting. "I'm scared, really scared this time," he admitted. "It feels different already."

"But that's all it is," Nini said. "Different. It's not necessarily bad."

"It's really hard to talk about," he said, looking at her. Being together was so comfortable and familiar. "I mean, not with you, but anyone else."

"You can talk with me about anything at any time, Ricky," she said. "I know things are kind of weird between us, but we're still friends. You know that."

They hugged, and in an awkward moment, Ricky leaned in a little more than he should have. It felt like they were going to kiss, but Nini jumped back and told him she would go get another pillow for him.

When she came back, Ricky was gone.

Ricky decided he needed to go home. His mom was still up when he arrived, packing up some boxes. She offered to make him something to eat. Ricky sank deep into the couch as she rustled around the kitchen. He slipped his earphones on to drown out the pain.

HOMECOMING

Based on the episode

by Tim Federle

Early in the morning, "Bop to the Top" blared through the speakers in the rehearsal room as Carlos and Seb danced the Sharpay-Ryan number. No one else was there, and they were enjoying a magic moment. They were perfectly in sync.

"Dancing with you is easy," Seb said. He admitted that dancing with the actor playing Ryan wasn't as easy, even though he practiced in his family's barn every night. "I need to practice with someone who actually knows how to lead."

Carlos took a drink from his water bottle. He was about to lead with a huge question. "Are you busy tonight?" he asked. "You know, homecoming?

Seb stared at Carlos. "You mean, like, you and I . . .

dancing together in front of all the non-theater kids?"

Carlos laughed. "As far as I know, that's how home-coming works. This would be my first time going." He held his breath. He knew this was a big leap.

Seb picked up his things to go and turned to Carlos. "Text me a pic of what you're wearing," he said as he walked out.

Carlos pumped his fist in the air. He had a date for homecoming!

Kourtney was concerned about Nini. She was in a stall in the girls' bathroom at school trying to flush her homecoming dress down a toilet! "Nini, baby," Kourtney said, "you need help!"

"You know what I need?" Nini said, as she took her dress out of the toilet and shoved it in the sink. "A girls' night!"

Just as they decided to forget about the home-coming dance, the last stall door in the bathroom flew open and Miss Jenn stood in front of them. "I'm in!" she exclaimed.

Miss Jenn was all about her cast, and she knew these girls needed a little something extra. She was ready to be there for them, and she had the perfect place in mind.

Ricky was surprised to see all the curtains closed and his dad lying on the living room couch in the middle of the afternoon.

"Why aren't you at rehearsal?" his dad asked, rubbing his eyes.

"Why aren't you at work?" Ricky countered.

"I'm taking a mental health day," he said.

"This is your fifth one in a row. That's like a mental health week." Ricky pulled the blanket away from his dad's face. "If Mom isn't coming back, this is the way it is now, okay?"

Ricky's dad groaned.

"I don't like it, either," Ricky said. "You need to take a shower and rejoin civilization."

His dad looked at him. "I don't see you exactly putting yourself out there post-breakup," he said.

Folding a blanket, Ricky grinned. "And that, good sir, is where you are wrong. I am going to homecoming tonight."

He wished he could say his date was Nini, since she was now single. Only he hadn't heard that from her. He had heard from Ashlyn, who heard it from Seb. But Ricky had a different kind of date. He was going with Big Red.

"We are in this together," Ricky told his dad. "Think of this as a bro-pact."

"Does this mean I need to make a dating profile?" Ricky's dad asked.

"First make your bed," Ricky joked. "Baby steps, Dad. Baby steps!"

Bonwood Bowling Alley was hopping when Nini, Kourtney, and Miss Jenn arrived. Families and tons of teens were bowling and having fun. Nini clapped her hands, excited for girls' night out. Only she knew that Kourtney and her well-manicured fingers would not want to bowl. Miss Jenn didn't seem so interested in bowling, either. She led the girls to the karaoke lounge in the back, where a guy was singing terribly, but proudly.

Miss Jenn grinned. "Tonight we are going to sit back and listen to some of Utah's worst vocalists." She wanted to boost Nini's confidence. "Look around. These people have half your talent, and twice your confidence."

"I am totally confident," Nini said. "Aren't I?"

"It takes time to step into the spotlight, Nini," Miss Jenn said. "That's why we are here tonight. Plus, I have a ten-year-old coupon for free sodas and nachos."

Miss Jenn left the girls at the table and went to the snack bar. Ricky's dad, Mike, was sitting at the bar and struck up a conversation. He tried to pretend he was waiting for someone, even though he wasn't. Miss Jenn intrigued him. She seemed to be interested, too. She was coy and took the sodas she ordered and headed to the back room.

While they waited for Miss Jenn, Nini glared at Gina's Instagram post from homecoming. Her date was E.J.! Kourtney wasn't really listening to Nini's rant, because across the room she saw Tonya Freeman. Even though Tonya had rejected all of Kourtney's costume ideas for the show, Tonya was wearing one of the outfits she had vetoed. Nini told her to go over and talk to Tonya, but Kourtney wasn't about to ruin girls' night.

Gina wasted no time in posting a photo of her and E.J. at the homecoming dance. There was no better way to let everyone know she was at the dance with E.J. Especially Nini. The thing was, Gina didn't really have a plan. Though she had convinced E.J. to take her to the dance, she really didn't know what she was doing. To E.J., she acted confident. "All will be revealed," she told him. "Just smile."

Before they even made it the theater kids' table, Big Red showed Ricky Gina's post. Ricky rolled his eyes. Not only had E.J. stolen his girlfriend, but the minute they broke up, he had a new date.

Carlos and Ashlyn were at the table, too. Carlos was also checking his phone.

"He'll show up," Ashlyn told him. "Don't assume Seb stood you up. Maybe he was in a farming accident."

"Not helping," Carlos said. He looked back at his blank screen. He wondered if Seb had chickened out.

"Can you get me some punch, babe?" Gina said to E.J.

"Sure, babe," E.J. said, playing the part.

When E.J. left the table, Ricky leaned over to Gina. He took the opportunity to tell Gina that E.J. was bad news and she could do better.

Gina didn't miss a beat. "You're not exactly one to give relationship advice," she spat.

"I sort of thought you were classier than this," Ricky said. "But maybe you really are what people say you are."

"And that is?" Gina asked.

Big Red's mouth dropped open. "Dude," he said, pulling on Ricky's arm. It wasn't like Ricky to be so mean. And that comment was a little out of line.

"A little too ambitious for your own good," Ricky told her.

Ricky and Big Red got up to walk around the dance. "Was this, like, a huge mistake?" Ricky asked.

"What? Calling Gina out like that?" said Big Red. "That was mad harsh, dude. You owe her an apology."

Ricky started to defend himself. "She showed up to the dance with my ex's ex. What's that about?"

Big Red shook his head. "Maybe not everything is about you. Maybe people are allowed to go out with whoever they want and be whoever they want to be." While he sounded a bit like a daytime self-help host, Big Red did actually make Ricky think. His thoughts, however, were interrupted by some drama at the punch table.

Gina and E.J. were arguing, and the animated conversation ended with Gina throwing a glass of punch at E.J.

Ricky followed Gina outside to the coat check. Gina fumbled with her coat ticket and turned to see him.

"You do not want to clap at me right now," she said. "I will clap back."

"Wait, I was . . . gonna apologize," Ricky said.

Gina took her coat. "Okay, go ahead," she told him.

"Oh, that was sort of it," he said, smiling at her. "I'm an outsider to the theater stuff, and you're an outsider to East High. I thought we sort of got each other."

This softened Gina, and Ricky looked a little more relaxed. "My world's been a little . . ." Ricky trailed off. "At home, too."

"You're not the only one with home drama," Gina

told him. She looked at Ricky. "Give me a ride home and we'll call it even."

Carlos went over to get some punch. Mr. Mazzara was serving, and Carlos confided in him. "My date didn't show up," he said. "I'm the fool who thought he'd actually dance in public with me."

Mr. Mazzara handed Carlos a glass of punch. "Well, the night's not over," he said. "We've all seen your moves. You don't need a dance partner to dance."

His unexpected and kind words gave Carlos the lift he needed. A new song came on, and Carlos started to tap his foot. As the song kicked into the chorus, Carlos headed out to the center of the dance floor.

E.J. whispered to Ashlyn, "I kinda feel bad for the guy."

Ashlyn looked at E.J., then got up to join her brave friend on the dance floor. She shadowed his moves, and before long everyone on the dance floor

Ricky panicked when Nini confessed her love on Instagram.

After a life-changing summer at drama camp, Nini felt ready to audition for the lead in East High's production of *High School Musical*.

Ashlyn shared the song she wrote for her character, Ms. Darbus, with Nini.

Tension was high between Ricky and E.J. as they ran lines for their roles as Troy and Chad.

forever...👎

Nini ended her romance with E.J. when she discovered he had stolen her phone.

Miss Jenn and Carlos watched as E.J. and Nini awkwardly sang a love song together.

Homecoming!

Nini tried to flush her homecoming dress down the toilet.

Instead of going to the dance, Kourtney, Nini, and Miss Jenn enjoyed a girls' night out at the bowling alley.

Gina convinced E.J. to take her to homecoming as part of her not-so-thought-out plan to make Nini and Ricky quit the play.

Miss Jenn defended herself at a school board hearing when it was discovered she had exaggerated the truth on her résumé.

Ricky and Nini started feeling confident in their roles as Troy and Gabriella as opening night drew near.

Kourtney and Big Red helped transport what was left of the play's costumes and props after the school theater fire.

Before the curtain went up, the cast and crew gathered for moment to celebrate.

Gina surprised everyone when she returned for opening night after a friend bought her a last-minute airline ticket.

Big Red proved his technical savvy on opening night, with a little help from Mr. Mazzara.

DON'T STICK TO THE STATUS QUO

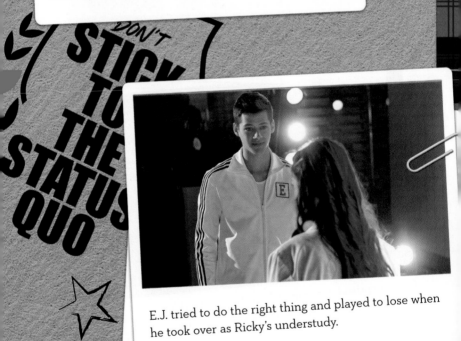

E.J. tried to do the right thing and played to lose when he took over as Ricky's understudy.

was dancing with Carlos. At the end of the song, the crowd of dancers lifted Carlos up and spun him around. When he landed, he laid eyes on Seb.

"Looks like I missed a lot," Seb said.

"The dance started three hours ago," Carlos told him.

"We lost one of our cows." Seb took a step closer to Carlos.

"You could have texted," Carlos said.

"We have bad cell reception at the barn. I'm really sorry about being so late."

"I'm really sorry about your cow," Carlos offered.

Seb smiled and took Carlos's hand. "At least our ties match."

A slow dance began, and the two headed to the center of the dance floor.

Miss Jenn returned to the table in the karaoke lounge and could see Nini and Kourtney were in the middle of something. She put the sodas down on the table and then went back out to the snack bar for the nachos. Mike was glad to see her again. He summoned enough courage to ask her out on a date—and for her name. Miss Jenn flirted, asking him if he wanted a stage name or a real name. She finally told him, and for the first time in a long time, she felt happy.

Meanwhile, Nini was trying to get Kourtney to stick up for herself and go over to speak to Tonya.

Kourtney sat up straight. "I didn't come here for a fight. I came to have fun."

The announcer called for "Nay Nay" to sing the next song.

"It's pronounced *Nee Nee*," Kourtney called. She turned to Nini. "Come on, this was our jam back in the day!" "Born to Be Brave" started playing, and Kourtney began to dance.

Nini wanted no part of performing. She felt like an imposter. She was not a singer or a lead in a show. The only reason she'd gotten the lead at camp was E.J.'s scheming. Her whole mission to be Nini 2.0 was based on a lie. She was a fraud. She headed for the door.

Kourtney followed her and passed Tonya on the way out. She took a deep breath. "Nice sweater," she said casually. Taking the high road felt empowering. She caught up with Nini outside in the alley.

"What happened to the seventh-grade Nini who used to belt out this song in the back seat of my mom's minivan?" Kourtney asked.

"She grew up," Nini mumbled.

Kourtney wasn't about to let Nini off so easily. "Ever since you discovered boys, you've spent *way* too much time seeing yourself through their eyes."

Nini got defensive, and then she paused. Maybe her friend was right.

"Miss Jenn is wrong," Kourtney told her. "You didn't lose your confidence. You just forgot why you loved to sing in the first place."

The beat of the song Kourtney had chosen for Nini to sing was pulsing through the door. Kourtney began to sing and Nini gave in to the music. This was a song she loved, and the two of them sang and danced. Nini realized it was the best feeling to reclaim her voice—and have a good time with her best friend.

After the song, they went back to the karaoke room and saw Miss Jenn. She looked a little different—more made up and all happy.

"Miss Jenn," Nini said, "did you meet someone in the bowling alley?"

Miss Jenn blushed. "It was a momentary flirtation," she said. "Trust me, men come and go, but girlfriends are forever."

They headed out to Miss Jenn's car. She asked the girls if they'd gotten what they came for that night. Nini and Kourtney laughed, and then Nini thought for a moment. "I think I might have gotten something better," she said.

Miss Jenn nodded and checked her phone. Principal Gutierrez had left a few messages for her. He had some information he wanted to discuss with her face to face. Miss Jenn kept her smile on and waved off Nini when she asked if everything was okay.

"Let's call it a night," she said, and pulled out of the lot.

"So this is where I live," Gina told Ricky as they pulled up in front of her house. "Let me guess—you pictured a wrought-iron gate and a bunch of gargoyles."

"You're not that scary," Ricky told her. Then he paused. "I kind of owe you a thank-you, actually."

"For what?" Gina asked.

Ricky reminded Gina of the conversation they'd had at the skate park. "You're the reason I stayed with the show. You set me straight," he said. "It's been a big deal for me. The Troy thing."

Gina smiled. "Well, it suits you," she said. She totally understood. Going to rehearsal after school had saved her, too.

"What was that big blowout with your date?" Ricky asked her.

She didn't really want to go into the whole mess with Ricky. It was hard enough to make friends, let alone have a successful date. "I kind of forgot about it already," she said. "I don't really date. Try moving five schools in seven years," she confessed.

"How is that working out for you?" Ricky asked.

Gina saw the porch lights flicker on and off. She had to go. Before she opened the door, she said, "I meant what I said at the skate park about you having your own style. I don't even think I knew how much I meant it when I said it. Good night, Ricky." She leaned over and gave him a kiss on the cheek.

The unexpected move took Ricky by surprise, but he kinda liked it.

WHAT TEAM?

Based on the episode
by Oliver Goldstick

Principal Gutierrez paced in Miss Jenn's office. "As you can see, this puts the administration in a very awkward position, which is why we have a process for this sort of thing," he told her. He had explained that the school board had received information that her résumé might have some inaccurate information. They had scheduled a meeting tomorrow to discuss it. He handed her a box and suggested that she pack up a few of her things.

Carlos stuck his head in Miss Jenn's office and asked if she was coming to the photo shoot. She knew she wasn't. She had to leave the building and would have to wait for the verdict from the school board.

But she smiled at Carlos and told him to start without her.

When Carlos returned to the auditorium, the cast was gathering onstage to take photos for the show's program. Everyone was in costume, and Nini was shocked to see Ricky looking all Zac Efron, complete with a straight-haired wig to frame his face.

"Oh my God, Ricky," she said, laughing. "I can't. There's so much to talk about."

"What's funny?" he said, sounding slightly offended.

Seb slipped on his silver bedazzled platform heels and slowly walked onto the stage. He adjusted his pink T-shirt, sequined vest, and cargo pants. Carlos saw him and went to check if he was okay.

"I don't know how to say this," Seb said, touching his pink highlights.

"Just say it," Carlos said with concern.

A smile spread across Seb's face. "I'm home," he said.

Big Red was ready with his camera. He wanted everyone to jump on cue to re-create the poster from the original *High School Musical*. His cues, however, were not working. Everyone was springing into the air at different times. Carlos called for a break.

E.J. found Gina in the corner and went over to her. "I'm a smidge confused," he said. "What happened to the plan? You made me take you to homecoming and then poured a drink on my head. . . ."

"Yeah," she said. "It was pretty complicated."

E.J. stared at her. "If there was ever a next step, I think I missed it. I'm still the understudy, and you seem pretty happy. What changed?"

"Nothing," Gina said, shrugging. "Everything? I don't know."

"I thought you wanted this as bad as I did," E.J. said.

"I thought I did," she said.

He looked at her. "Do you care about Ricky now?"

"What if I do?" she asked.

"Um, guys," Carlos said, breaking up the conversation.

"Not now!" Gina and E.J. barked in unison.

Carlos shrank away and called Miss Jenn. He thought she was joking when she told him she might be out of a job in twenty-four hours, but as he turned the corner in the school hallway, he saw her carrying her box of things.

"Oh my God!" Carlos said. "What happened?"

"I may have exaggerated one or two credits on my résumé," she said. "The important thing is you keep this train on the tracks. Hopefully everything will be cleared up when I sit before the school board tomorrow."

Then she told him to keep rehearsal going and not tell any of the cast. "In the theater, morale is everything," she said as she was escorted out by Principal Gutierrez. Looking back over her shoulder, she caught Carlos's eyes. "Trust the process!" she said.

Back in the auditorium, the cast was wondering where Miss Jenn and Carlos were. As they waited, Big Red quizzed Ricky about his night with Gina, but Ricky wasn't divulging anything. He only confessed to not being sure about what was happening.

"Should I just live vicariously through someone else?" Big Red asked.

"Okay, people!" Carlos cried when he entered the auditorium. "Let's stage a number!" He explained that Miss Jenn had a small personal matter and wouldn't be there.

"Is everything all right?" Nini asked.

"Everything is fine," Carlos barked. "Why would you even ask that?"

His defensive response put everyone on edge.

Carlos continued with his idea for staging Gabriella's song, "When There Was Me and You." He wanted each of the male cast members to stand on a box, and Gabriella would wander through this forest of boys as she sang. This idea didn't make sense to Nini. After all, Troy had just sold Gabriella out to his teammates. Why would she be singing to these boys or trees?

Ashlyn agreed with Nini. "She's got a point," she told Carlos. "What Troy did was kind of unforgivable. The last thing anyone wants in this moment is four more versions of him."

Kourtney spoke up, too. "Maybe she's surrounded by a forest of loving and supportive sisters!"

The cast began to take sides, and Ricky held up his hand. "Is it better if she just sings a solo acoustic version?"

Gina smiled and voted for Ricky's idea, but Carlos snapped. "This is not a democracy!"

Carlos's outburst was a little surprising. Nini stepped closer to him. "Are you okay? We could just wait for Miss Jenn."

"Miss Jenn's not here, and I don't know if she's ever coming back!" he exclaimed.

Now the cast was silent. Carlos explained that Miss Jenn was in trouble because she had lied on her job application and could be fired. She had to wait for the school board meeting tomorrow. The news made everyone upset and tense.

"I need a minute," Nini said and walked out with Kourtney.

A few other cast members started to pack up their stuff, too.

"Rehearsals are officially cancelled until further notice," Carlos said.

In the hallway, Carlos confronted Mr. Mazzara.

"Benjamin Mazzara. I assume you know what's happening to Miss Jenn," Carlos said.

"I may have heard a rumor in the faculty lounge," he said.

"The real question is, who narced on Miss Jenn?" Carlos said accusatorially.

"Are you suggesting that I had something to do with this?" he responded.

"Are you admitting that you did?" Carlos responded.

"Of course not," Mr. Mazzara told Carlos. "Look, kid, has it occurred to you that Miss Jenn is responsible for her own untimely demise?"

E.J. raced down the hallway, looking for Nini.

"Miss Jenn isn't the only person with secrets," he

confessed when he found his ex-girlfriend. "Look, I really need to get some things off my chest."

He began to confess his plot to steal the part of Troy from Ricky and win Nini back. Then, he went on to apologize to Nini for all he had done—though Nini wasn't sure why. "Why are you telling me this all now?" she asked.

"It's over, Nini," he said. "The show. My parents used to be on the school board. If there's a hearing tomorrow, Miss Jenn is a done deal." He watched Nini's face. "I'm sorry you won't get to be Gabriella. The audience doesn't know what they're missing . . . but I do."

His words sank in fast, and Nini was crushed. After E.J. left, she heard Ricky singing down the hall. She peeked inside the rehearsal room and saw him playing guitar and singing "When There Was Me and You." And then she spotted Gina. She and Ricky were staring into each other's eyes—and Nini backed away.

Ricky didn't see Nini because he was looking at Gina as he sang and played guitar. He hoped she liked his version of the song. There was definitely some flirting happening here, and it felt good. It also felt good to be singing, which took Ricky a little by surprise. He had started to really enjoy performing.

"Should we be doing something? Like to help Miss Jenn," he said after he finished his song.

Carlos slipped into a booth at the coffeehouse and sat across from Miss Jenn. She told her loyal assistant that everything that would be said about her at the school board hearing was true. She was a fake teacher. She pushed her red file box toward Carlos. It was her director's files and staging ideas. "It's for your next teacher," she said, standing up. "I just hope she loves you guys half as much as I do."

Carlos was speechless and incredibly sad. He checked his phone and saw that the cast was at Big Red's. He headed over there and found everyone sitting around the basement commiserating. Carlos broke the silence. "I'm mad at Miss Jenn," he said.

"Because she has some skeletons in her closet?" Gina asked.

"No," Carlos replied. "Because she's giving up." He looked around at the cast. "She gave me a shot, and it's been a long time since someone gave me a shot."

Ashlyn was thoughtful for a moment. "Does anyone here actually care if her past is a little bit sketchy?"

"I do," Ricky said.

Everyone turned to look at him.

"What, because you've lived some perfect life?" Kourtney asked.

Ricky sat up straighter. "Not at all," he said. "Because she put our show in jeopardy. And now we are here, and maybe for the last time. And for some of us, this has become . . ."

"A family," Nini finished for him.

"Okay, Wildcats. So what are we doing about it?" Ashlyn asked.

Miss Jenn was sitting on a bench outside East High waiting for the school board meeting to begin when she saw Ricky's dad, Mike. One of the cast members called out her name, and Mike was surprised to learn she was the Miss Jenn he had been hearing about. She was shocked to discover Mike was Ricky's dad. They shared an awkward moment. "Let's talk after, maybe?" Miss Jenn said.

The school board meeting was held in the cafeteria. Principal Gutierrez began the proceedings by asking Miss Jenn about the charges. "There is news that your résumé was exaggerated," he said. "Your teaching credentials may have been from an obscure online university, and even your official name could be a version of your stage name. What do you say to these charges?"

As Miss Jenn was speaking, Nini and Ricky stood at the door, directing the cast to seats. Very soon, the cafeteria was filled with the whole cast.

Carlos looked over his shoulder and saw Mr. Mazzara watching from the stairway.

"I have always done my best by these kids," Miss Jenn said.

"Excuse me," Mike said, standing up. "Can I say something?"

The principal allowed him to have the floor.

"The real crime here would be booting a teacher who's making a positive impact," Mike said. "I've never seen my kid this invested in anything. And I don't think that's something we should punish."

Principal Gutierrez began to speak, but was distracted by humming. He looked up to the cafeteria landing and saw Kourtney holding a boom box over her head. Kourtney and Nini led the song "Truth, Justice & Songs in Our Key," and everyone in the cast took a verse. The words complimented Miss Jenn and her work on the musical—and everything she had done for her students. Soon everyone was dancing on the tables and the meeting turned into a dance party. At the end, everyone applauded.

"Do we have any further questions?" Principal Gutierrez asked. The only question was about getting tickets for opening night! "This meeting is adjourned," the beaten-down principal said.

Ricky caught his dad and Miss Jenn sharing a moment across the room. His dad had saved her and the show with his speech, but had he known Miss Jenn before that day?

THANKSGIVING

Based on the episode

by Ann Kim

The day before Thanksgiving break, the cast was running through the song "Start of Something New." Nini and Ricky sounded great together. Nini was really impressed by how hard Ricky had worked. He had really pulled himself together and was confident in the leading role. Though he seemed to always be looking at Gina.

"Your homework over this break is to please go on vocal rest," Miss Jenn said. "And go over your lines, too, which is hard to do on vocal rest, but make it work." She smiled at her students. "And may nothing ever block your doorway to happiness."

Mr. Mazzara walked into the rehearsal room and handed Ashlyn a thick binder from the robotics club.

Ashlyn was super involved in almost every club at school, but the robotics club? Big Red's eyes widened. He had no idea. It only made him have more respect for her.

Carlos listened to Mr. Mazzara and Miss Jenn talk about their family Thanksgiving meals with peach cobbler and candied yams. He leaned over to Big Red. "My family usually has three protein courses, and then everyone is asleep by six," he said.

Big Red nodded. "My folks start eating at dawn, and they barely make it past the Macy's parade," he said.

Ashlyn joined in the conversation. She told them her parents were going to a spa with E.J.'s parents. Just then, she had a great idea. "Do you guys want to come over after dinner tomorrow, like a late-night party?"

Before Big Red could ask if they should open up the invite to the whole cast or not, Carlos blurted out to the room that Ashlyn was hosting a party. Everyone seemed psyched to go.

This was the first holiday that was just Ricky and his dad—and it felt strange. His dad told him to call his mom. "She really misses you, Ricky," he said. "She's all alone in Chicago, and she is waiting for you to call." Ricky wasn't sure what to say to his mom. His dad, however, was letting him off the hook on attending the family gathering at his aunt's house later. Ricky had told him he was planning on going to Ashlyn's party.

"I suppose if you're lonely, you could just randomly text my drama teacher," Ricky joked with his dad.

"Too soon, Rick," Mike said with a laugh.

Once his dad left, Ricky picked up the phone to call his mom. Only a man answered. Ricky quickly recovered and said, "I was trying to reach Lynne. I think I have the wrong number."

"No, you got it right," the man said. "Ricky, this is Todd. I have heard so much about you. Lynne is in the shower. Can I take a message?"

Ricky felt like he had been punched in the

stomach. Who was Todd? And why did he know so much about him? Ricky hung up fast. His first instinct was to call Nini. But things with Nini had been kind of weird, so he rethought the impulse. A knock at the door brought him out of his trance. Gina was standing at his front door holding some cupcakes decorated like turkeys.

"Gina, hi," he said. "Come in."

"Thanks. I thought I could walk you to Ashlyn's, but it's kind of freezing out, so I made you this hat," she said, handing him a knit cap.

Ricky was impressed.

"You spend enough time alone in the house, and you pick up all sorts of crafts on YouTube," she told him.

"Sorry, can I meet you there?" he asked.

Gina realized something was going on with Ricky. "Is everything okay?"

"No," Ricky confessed. "I guess my mom has a new boyfriend, and it's just a lot. I'm sorry. I hate to be a downer."

"Look, I get it," Gina said.

"No offense, but I'm not sure you do," he said.

Gina sighed. The truth was she did understand. "Let me guess: you're mad at everyone and everything because just when you're getting used to things changing, they change again."

Ricky stared at Gina. How did she nail his feelings so well?

"Ricky," Gina continued, "I'm not sure you noticed, but my family is just me and my mom. She's at FEMA, so we basically move whenever disaster strikes. I've had a few feelings in my life."

Embarrassed, Ricky realized how wrong he had been about Gina. "Of course, yeah," he said. "I'm sorry."

"Don't be," Gina said. "I'm just saying, you just gotta ignore it and push through." She smiled at him.

"Do you think I should text her 'Happy Thanksgiving' or something?" he asked.

Gina shrugged. "What I think we should do is go to the party and spend a few hours being drama dorks." She laughed. "But do what makes you happy."

Ricky took Gina's handmade hat and put it on. And with that, they headed out the door to Ashlyn's house.

Big Red showed up at Ashlyn's early to help her set up for the party. Ashlyn had been wondering how he got involved with the show. He didn't really seem like a crew kind of guy. Big Red told her it was because of Ricky. He was being a good friend and giving Ricky moral support because Nini was dating E.J.

"Sorry, I forgot you guys were related," Big Red told her.

"Well, hey, I promise not to steal your phone if you promise not to throw a basketball at my face."

Big Red set the soda down on the table and looked over at Ashlyn. "The only thing I'd ever throw at your face is a brighter spotlight, because I like the way you sing."

Ashlyn grinned. That was such a nice compliment it made her face flush.

Before the family sat down to Thanksgiving dinner, Nini's grandmother was entertaining her with stories about when she had first come to America. Nini was inspired hearing her grandmother talk about when she'd been Nini's age and had a chance to start over when her family moved to the United States. The idea of starting over somewhere new was very exciting to Nini—and it made her think.

When Nini arrived at Ashlyn's party, most of the cast were there already. She went to the kitchen to help Ashlyn prep snacks for everyone. She really liked Ashlyn and admired her songwriting talents.

"'Wondering' is literally the best ballad in the show, and I'm low-key jealous that Gabriella doesn't get to sing it," Nini told her. "I wish I could write like that."

Ashlyn appreciated the compliment but felt a little embarrassed by the attention. "Okay, but didn't you write that completely adorkable song about how you don't not love someone?" Ashlyn said.

"That was a onetime thing, and it totally backfired," Nini said. "I highly recommend not telling someone you love them for the first time on Instagram."

"Maybe you should write something for yourself, then," Ashlyn said, encouraging her.

Carlos came into the living room holding a very long box. He had brought a homemade board game he'd made many years ago, High School Musical: The Choosical.

"When I was a child, I wanted to go into the movie, but the movie was on-screen, so I decided to create the next best thing: an interactive, hyperactive HSM experience that could be played by children and adults everywhere in the world," he said.

"Wait," Big Red said. "You've had this for ten years?"

"Actually," Carlos said, "I never played it."

"We'll totally play it," Ashlyn told him.

Carlos explained there were two teams: the East High Wildcats and the West High Knights. The cast split up into teams. Ashlyn watched Big Red move to the Knights and joined him on that team.

E.J. arrived holding a large dish of lobster dip. He was eager to tell Ashlyn about his confessional Instagram posts. He had committed to being a better person and was starting by publicly stating all his bad deeds and schemes on his social media sites. He was FaceTiming with Emily Pratt from drama camp when he arrived. "Hold on one sec," he said to Emily. "I've just gotta find Nini."

As if on cue, Nini moved through the crowd and saw Emily on E.J.'s screen.

"Oh my God, Emily," Nini said.

E.J. grinned. "It's okay," he said. "She knows all about the deviled egg! I'm making amends these days, Nini, and she was fine with everything. She laughed!"

"Wow," Nini said.

"Hey, I gotta go join the party," E.J. told her. "And

admit some terrible things." He handed the phone to Nini. "You ladies catch up!"

Nini felt so awkward. "I am . . . so sorry about what happened this summer," she said.

"That's all so far in the rearview I can't even tell you," Emily said. "Water under the bridge. I started at this new boarding school for the arts and it's everything. Seriously makes all that stuff last summer feel like kindergarten."

"Oh, wow," Nini replied.

"There's nothing like a fresh start to completely stretch your talent," Emily said.

Emily cut the conversation short, and Nini took a minute to digest what had just happened. Just then, Ricky came in the front door.

"Hey, look who's here," Nini said.

"I didn't know if you'd make it," Ricky said.

"I'd figured I'd check in with all my . . . buddies," she joked, not really knowing what to call him.

"Nice," Ricky said. "We heard a rumor that Carlos went off the deep end and we didn't want to miss it."

"We?" Nini asked.

And then Gina came in the door behind Ricky. She was holding the gluten-free turkey cupcakes she had made from a recipe on YouTube.

"Again with you and YouTube," Ricky said, and he shared a giggle with Gina.

Nini eyed them. Now they had inside jokes! They were a "we" now?

Luckily, Carlos called the game to order. He explained how his game had trivia and singing and dance challenges that all related to *High School Musical*. The cast was up for the challenge.

First the Knights had to sing the lyrics of "What I've Been Looking For" to the rhythm of "Get'cha Head in the Game." This sent everyone into a fit of giggles. The next challenge went to E.J. and Ricky. They had to stare at each other doing the Sharpay and Ryan warm-up for sixty seconds straight without laughing.

Nini ducked out of the room for a root beer refill at the same time as Gina. In the kitchen, Gina confided that always being the new girl had been hard for her, but she had high hopes for junior year at East High. When Gina tried to apologize for all the drama she had caused as the wonderstudy, Nini stopped her. "It's all good," Nini said. Then she changed the subject. "You're staying over tonight, right?"

Gina had never been invited to a sleepover before. With all the times she and her mom had moved, making friends was really hard. But here, she felt a part of something. And she liked that feeling.

Back out in the living room, the board game was still going on and the score was tied. It was time for a rapid trivia play-off. Gina got the winning answer, and Carlos gave her a homemade scholastic decathlon ribbon. Feeling really happy, Gina called her mom on speakerphone. When her mom asked to be taken off speaker, everyone knew something was up. Gina's mom told her that they would be moving again . . . in ten days. Gina had been having such a great time, but now her night was ruined. She grabbed her cupcake pan from the kitchen and was about to bolt when Ricky stopped her.

"Do you want to talk about it?" he asked.

"Not even a little," Gina said. "Honestly, you heard what happened. I don't think there's any point in calling me anymore, do you?" She turned and left Ashlyn's house.

Ricky followed her to the door, but Gina was gone.

"Hey, are you all right?" Nini asked, moving closer to him. "That was pretty intense."

"Yeah, I was there," Ricky spat.

Nini tried to say something comforting, but Ricky bristled. "It's not just Gina," he said. "My mom moved out two weeks ago and she's already got a new boyfriend. Sound familiar?"

Nini backed up. "Whoa," she said. "You can be mad at me all you want, but you should talk to your mom."

"Thanks, but I really don't need more advice from my *buddy* right now," he said, and walked out the door.

Everyone started to clear out of Ashlyn's house. After Gina's crushing news, none of the girls were in the mood for a sleepover. Big Red was the only one who stayed to help Ashlyn clean up. He saw Ashlyn's piano and asked her if this was where she had written that Sara Bareilles song about regrets for Ms. Darbus.

"Did someone tell you to say that? Because that's all I've wanted to hear my entire life," Ashlyn said, completely touched by Big Red comparing her song to one of her favorite singer's.

"I should go," Big Red said.

Ashlyn thanked him and then gave him the leftover lobster dip.

Miss Jenn and Mr. Mazzara were surprised to find each other in the faculty lounge at East High on Thanksgiving. They both came clean about their non-existent family Thanksgiving dinners and their school projects. Mr. Mazzara was working on a robot, and Miss Jenn was working on how to get Troy to levitate onstage. She was trying to figure out the maneuver using a Troy doll wrapped in string.

Miss Jenn eyed Mr. Mazzara's work for the Roboticon. "You want some help?" she asked.

Mr. Mazzara puffed out his chest. "I am an engineer by trade, Miss Jenn," he said. "I think I've got it." But he clearly didn't. His robot kept falling over.

"Okay," Miss Jenn told him. "The center of gravity is off, and if that was a dancer, she'd be in traction." She turned and walked away.

"Wait." He sighed. "How would you fix it?"

Taking her time, Miss Jenn manipulated the robot and, in a few moves, solved the balance issue. Mr. Mazzara was impressed.

"Honey, it's called a plié," she said.

In return, Mr. Mazarra did some quick calculations and was able to figure out a pulley system for the Troy levitation. He demonstrated the pulley with the doll for Miss Jenn.

"It's beautiful," she gushed, beaming at him.

"Math often is," he said.

"Benjamin, I'm going to cry," Miss Jenn said, getting teary-eyed.

"Please don't," he told her. "I can't stress to you enough how uncomfortable that would make me feel."

"You did something nice for me," Miss Jenn gushed. "You know what we should do? When I was young, my family used to do a movie night on Thanksgiving. You wanna?"

At first, Mr. Mazzara declined, but Miss Jenn offered up *Big Hero 6*, which she knew would grab his attention and his robot-loving mind.

They heated up some leftovers and made some tea, then sat down on the couch to watch. Before the movie ended, Miss Jenn and Mr. Mazzara were asleep. While they slept, in the corner of the room, the plug from the teapot began to spark in the socket. Fast asleep, they didn't notice—or smell—the start of a fire.

THE TECH
REHEARSAL

Based on the episode
by Natalia Castells-Esquivel

When Nini arrived at school after Thanksgiving break, she couldn't believe her eyes. The cast was standing in front of yellow caution tape strung across the East High theater.

"Oh my gosh, what happened?" Nini asked.

Miss Jenn came out from backstage. "It's okay," she told them. "Nobody was hurt. There was a small fire in the theater over the holiday, and the sprinklers did their job."

A firefighter followed Miss Jenn. "We're almost done in here," she said. "We have to finish up in the faculty lounge next. Some circuits blew in there over break."

Miss Jenn gulped. She and Mr. Mazzara had

fallen asleep in the lounge on Thanksgiving. They had smelled smoke. Benjamin Mazzara had said to run, so she ran. She would donate her salary if she had to, but the show must go on!

"Unfortunately, the show can't go on," the firefighter said.

"What?" Miss Jenn said, turning around.

The firefighter shook her head. "The fire ripped through all the costumes, and the sprinklers ruined all your sets." She shrugged. "I'm sorry. We're gonna have to red-tag the entire backstage area for at least a month."

"Did she just say costumes?" Kourtney gasped. Her costumes were gone?

Miss Jenn told the kids they would reconvene in the cafeteria after school to talk about their options. She looked to Nini and Ricky to take on the responsibility of spreading the word, since they were the show leads. Nini rose to the task, but Ricky seemed preoccupied with his phone. He had been texting Gina all morning. He hadn't spoken to her since her big news about moving.

At the cafeteria meeting, Miss Jenn asked where Gina was. "She's going through a family thing right now," Ashlyn explained.

"If we don't have a theater, we don't have a show," Miss Jenn told the group. "I guess we could consider other venues." She didn't quite know what that meant, but she needed to find a new theater for the show.

"How about the El Rey?" Carlos asked. The old theater was for sale and had once been a major attraction downtown. His uncle was the listing agent. Carlos thought the idea was perfect, yet Miss Jenn seemed to be having a very weird reaction to his suggestion.

"I can't imagine we'd be able to get in on such short notice," Miss Jenn told Carlos.

Carlos was two steps ahead and already had his uncle on the phone. He agreed to have the show at the El Rey. Everyone cheered except Miss Jenn. "Aren't you excited?" Carlos asked her.

Miss Jenn put on her theater face and nodded, though inside she was crumbling. The El Rey was the theater where the original *High School Musical* had premiered. And that was not a night she wanted to revisit.

The cast started to load up props, boxes, and lights from backstage to take over to the El Rey.

Kourtney stood in the hallway and watched Ashlyn and Seb laughing as they awkwardly carried a long light board out of the auditorium. "Looks like the cast is in pretty good spirits," she said to Big Red.

"Yeah," he agreed. "Actors, man. Fire or no fire, they've still got their charm and perfect skin."

Kourtney chuckled. "I know it's silly, but I feel like I lost a little piece of myself when all those costumes went up in flames."

Big Red agreed. After all, he had spent weeks on the papier-mâché basketball that had been ruined in the fire.

As Carlos walked by, Kourtney asked him if there

was any emergency money to replace some of the costumes.

"Let's just stick a pin in that, Kourt," he said. "Right now the priority is making sure we can put up a show." He continued to walk down the hall and saw E.J. with Miss Jenn's red file box. "Oh, hey," he called. "Maybe I should carry that. It's just a little bit sensitive. It's Miss Jenn's show file, with her script breakdown, set sketches, and audition notes."

"You mean this says why which people got which parts?" E.J. asked.

"No further comment," Carlos said, grabbing the box and running down the hall.

Nini and Kourtney walked into the El Rey holding flashlights. The dark old theater was a little creepy.

"How are you holding up?" Kourtney asked Nini.

Shrugging, Nini confessed, "I actually feel weirdly guilty. Almost like I caused this. Like it's a sign."

Kourtney smiled at her. "How could you have caused this?"

"I had kind of a strange weekend," she said. "I started thinking about applying to this performing arts school."

As Nini explained to Kourtney about Youth Actors Conservatory, she felt more certain about needing to "find new shores," as her grandmother had when she came to America.

"You were going to spend senior year without me," Kourtney said, sounding really hurt.

Then Nini looked around at the cast trying to get the stage ready. "But that's over now," she said. "We have a show to save."

"Yeah," Kourtney said. "For sure." And she watched Nini rush onstage to join the others.

E.J. found Miss Jenn's red file box and took it into the stairwell. His confessional posts hadn't really helped him or his reputation. His followers were dropping off, and no one seemed very interested in his honesty plan. He decided that he just had to be himself. And he wanted to read his audition file to find out why Miss Jenn had cast Ricky instead of him. As he flipped through the notes, he smiled at Miss Jenn's comment: "Classic Troy on paper." His grin disappeared when he scrolled down the page. "Lacks an emotional connection to the material." E.J. was stumped. Now he was committed to proving her wrong.

Onstage, Miss Jenn was trying to get the tech rehearsal going. Though the theater barely even had lights, she urged everyone to take their places and called for Natalie Bagley, the stage manager, to start.

Seb stepped forward. "Um, Natalie Bagley's getting her wisdom teeth out," he said.

Miss Jenn sighed. "Okay, so I'm down a stage manager and my Taylor is M.I.A."

Ricky jumped in. "Gina's okay. She's a fighter, and she'll be back for opening night."

"She texted you?" Nini asked.

"No," Ricky said. "You?"

Nini shook her head.

A large sandbag fell from the rafters. Miss Jenn shuddered. Maybe this place was haunted, and not only by her memories of the premiere. She took a deep breath and called the cast for "Stick to the Status Quo" onstage. She then sent Nini and Ricky to find somewhere quiet to rehearse their rooftop scene. They'd hardly spoken since Ashlyn's party, so it was a little awkward, but they followed Miss Jenn's directions.

Before Ashlyn took her place onstage, she saw Big Red in the wings holding a light. "Hey, you okay?" she asked.

"Yeah," Big Red said. "I just don't know how to make things light up."

"You walk into a room," Ashlyn said.

Big Red blushed. "Oh, you," he said.

Ashlyn smiled. "Seriously, I've been through a few tech rehearsals in my day. Just holler if you need me."

"Thanks, Ash," Big Red said.

Before walking onstage, she turned to him. "You got this."

Big Red grinned.

Nini and Ricky found a creepy storage room for some privacy to read through their scene. Before they got started, Ricky wanted to talk about what had happened at Ashlyn's party.

"It was totally fine," Nini said. "I get it."

"Do you?" Ricky asked.

"I meant I said something nice," Nini told him. "You acted like a punk. What is there to discuss?"

Ricky couldn't let that go without talking it out. "For the record," he said, "you're the one who called me your buddy, and I've been iced out for weeks, so maybe it was building up." He flipped through his script to find the scene.

"Okay. Glad you got that out of your system?" Nini said sarcastically. "Page fifty-three?"

"Yeah, actually, I am," Ricky replied. "Page fifty-three. I'm all about the work."

As they went through the scene, Ricky read the line about kindergarten, and it reminded him of when he and Nini were five. He was the one who'd come up with her nickname because he couldn't say Nina. "I still can't think of you as a Nina," he said.

"You could just call me buddy," she said, smiling.

"For the record," he said, "I was Richard Bowen until first grade, when you started calling me Ricky."

Nini knew he was right. But no one under fifty should be called Richard!

More memories were flooding in, and they laughed about microwaving a Barbie, a moldy-bread science experiment, and that song about how Nini loved him . . . though that last one was a little too soon. Or not.

"Maybe we should warm up our voices in case we have to sing later," she said, changing the subject.

Meanwhile, back onstage, Miss Jenn was trying to get the lighting right for the rooftop scene. She asked for volunteers to help.

"I can do Troy," E.J. said. Then, under his breath, he muttered, "Or at least some people think so."

"Fine," Miss Jenn called. "Carlos, you stand in for Gabriella."

A flood of green lights hit the stage. Carlos explained there had been a fashion show there previously, but the green was more like a nuclear reactor and the backdrop was some kind of bizarre ancient ruins. Miss Jenn exhaled deeply.

"Big Red!" Miss Jenn yelled. "Do we have anything more flattering?'

"I'm working on it!" he replied.

E.J. continued reading Troy's lines, laying on the emotion thick. Even though he was reading through the lines with Carlos, he read the lines as if he were really falling for Gabriella.

"That's excellent," Miss Jenn said. "And a little weird." She called to Big Red. "Any progress?"

"I think I found it!" Big Red replied.

The stage went dark, and then black lights lit up the stage with an eerie glow.

Miss Jenn called for E.J. and Carlos to go on with the scene. E.J. continued to ramp up the emotion and even had tears in his eyes.

"E.J., are you sick?" Miss Jenn asked.

Carlos knew exactly what happened. He knew E.J. had read the audition notes. When he approached him, E.J. was defensive. Laying the emotion on too thick wasn't good either, Carlos explained to him.

"I need a volunteer to sing into the microphone for sound check," Miss Jenn called out.

"Kourtney's an amazing singer," one of the dancers said.

"Singer, not actor," Kourtney said. "This voice is for church."

After professing that this was a safe space, Miss Jenn got Kourtney up onstage. She sang "Bop to the Top" a cappella and shocked everyone with her amazing voice.

"Kourtney, honey," Miss Jenn gushed, "that was a *wow*." She looked around at the rest of the cast. "Unfortunately, it seems we have now broken the sound system, the lights, and possibly me. Carlos, could you please clear the theater right now?"

"Miss Jenn, are you okay?" Carlos asked. He saw

Miss Jenn's face and knew he had to obey her orders. "Everyone follow me. We're on a long five."

Ashlyn went back into the theater and saw Miss Jenn stroking a theater seat. "Miss Jenn," she said carefully, "I don't think I'm alone in noticing that you seem fully freaked out."

Miss Jenn smiled at Ashlyn. "This is where I was sitting," she said. "The Utah premiere of *High School Musical*." She remembered that the whole row was filled with family and friends. "I only cared about Lucas Grabeel," she said with a sigh. "He played Ryan." He had called her Jessica instead of Jennifer, but she didn't have the heart to tell him her real name. Miss Jenn went on to explain she'd had one line in the cafeteria scene. "Is that the last apple?" was her big moment, but it was cut from the movie. Lucas was the only lead who told her she'd nailed it. "That night set me back seven years," Miss Jenn said. "My confidence was shattered."

Ashlyn nodded. "Wow, that's terrible," she said.

She wanted to boost her teacher up. "You know, you inspired me to write a whole song about regrets."

"I know," Miss Jenn said. "And nobody will ever hear it, because our PA system died faster than my career in New York."

Knowing she had to do something, Ashlyn handed her teacher a set of three crystals. "Use them," she said. "Trust yourself the way we all trust you."

Miss Jenn held the crystals in her hand. She did some positive affirmations and walked up onstage. "I can still pull off this show," she said to herself. "Somehow." She lifted a tarp and saw a mannequin resembling Ryan from the original movie. She felt dizzy and fainted. When she opened her eyes, she was face to face with the real Lucas Grabeel! He looked like her guardian angel. He told her to let the cut line memory go and move on. And he had a song for her . . . and the inspired idea to have the show in the East High gym.

In the storage room, Nini and Ricky were warming up their voices. Nini told Ricky she was thinking about a drama school in Denver, though the school was very hard to get into and she didn't think they'd take her.

"But you're, like, one-in-a-million talented," Ricky told her.

Nini laughed. "You don't know how much talent is out there."

When Ricky began to praise Nini, she felt a little uncomfortable and tried to change the subject.

"That's not fair," Ricky joked. "My parents took me to Disneyland once, and I met a very talented Minnie Mouse."

"Ah, yes, your first crush," Nini said.

"Actually, she was my second," Ricky admitted. The two looked at each other, and just as they were about to kiss, Big Red pushed the door open and asked if they wanted pizza. The moment surprised them both—and then it passed. They joined Big Red and the others in the lobby.

Kourtney spotted Nini and sensed something

was up with her. Nini was about to tell her about the almost kiss, but just confessed she had almost done something really stupid. She changed the subject and praised Kourtney for singing onstage. She knew her friend had the best voice at school. Kourtney admitted to liking the applause, and she understood why Nini loved performing. When Nini walked away, Kourtney took out her phone and called Youth Actors Conservatory. If Nini wasn't going to put herself out there, then Kourtney would do it for her.

Carlos was stress-eating popcorn from the concession stand when E.J. found him.

"Hey, it's been a long time since we went on break," E.J. said. "Should we go ask what's going on?"

"She's having a moment," Carlos said. "Maybe you can go and ask her."

"I don't want to freak her out more with my lifeless eyes," E.J. joked.

"You were right, by the way," Carlos told E.J. "Forest of Boys was a mess, and coming here was a huge mistake. I have no business taking charge of anything."

E.J. disagreed. "You stepped up, dude," he told him. "You always do, and if I'm being honest, it's admirable."

"E.J., was that a compliment?" Carlos asked.

"Don't make me start emoting," he joked.

"Okay, well, the words were a four, but the sentiment was a solid ten," Carlos told him.

E.J. grinned and walked away.

Carlos went into the theater and panicked when he saw Miss Jenn lying on the stage. He rushed over to her and slapped her awake. "Miss Jenn! Say something!" he begged.

Miss Jenn came to, realized where she was, and sighed. "I'm the teacher, and we're making history," she said. "Everything's gonna be okay."

"We can't use the theater," he told her. "The principal said we can't use an outside facility for a school event."

"I know where we have to go," Miss Jenn said, sitting up. "Back to East High."

CHAPTER

09

OPENING NIGHT

Based on the episode

by Oliver Goldstick

Big Red got Ricky's message and rushed over to his house. He found Ricky singing a song that he had written about falling in love. Only Big Red wasn't sure if Ricky had written the song for Nini or Gina. Big Red thought the song was great, but he had been working nonstop to re-create the sets for the show and was exhausted. Ricky confessed that he had almost kissed Nini and had written her the song for opening night.

Ricky didn't know that Nini was also thinking of giving him an opening night gift. Nini showed Kourtney engraved dog tags that she had made for Ricky. And she also confessed to almost kissing him.

Kourtney had some news, too. Miss Jenn had asked her to take on the role of Taylor now that Gina was gone. Nini was thrilled for her friend to join her onstage. But she was still nervous about opening night. She went early to East High and was surprised to find Ricky there, too.

"Let me guess," Ricky said when he saw her. "Jitters?"

"A little bit," Nini replied. "I realized this morning that this is the first time I've been cast as the lead on purpose."

Miss Jenn came up behind her and put her hand on Nini's shoulder. "But it won't be the last," she said. She encouraged her two leads to soak in the stillness before the opening.

However, Natalie and Big Red were making lots of noise trying to finish setting the stage. Nini and Ricky ducked out into the hallway to get some quiet.

"Um, the other night, when we were in that room at the theater," Nini began. She was hesitant about bringing up the almost kiss. And Ricky took her comment the wrong way. He suddenly felt as if he had to backtrack his plan.

"Oh, listen," he said, trying to act cool, "that was a tough day. We were all in a really weird place."

"Yeah," Nini agreed. "Totally weird."

"We're cool, right?" Ricky asked.

Nini thought about the gift she had for him. Maybe it was all show-mance and nothing more.

Later, the cast gathered for hair and makeup. Carlos was carrying a large bouquet of flowers. "We've got mystery flowers, people!" he called. There was no card, and no one took credit for sending them. "We'll have to share them," Miss Jenn said. Then she shared some other news. She told the cast that Gina sent her love and support but was already on the East Coast. "And so I have asked Kourtney to fill in," she said.

Everyone cheered for Kourtney. She held a bound script in her hand and grinned at Nini.

"Please think of a word or phrase from the show that expresses where your head is or your goals for tonight," Miss Jenn told the cast.

Big Red went first. "'You're my guys, and this is our team,'" he said.

"'What if you wanna try something really new and it's a total disaster and all your friends laugh at you?'" Ricky said, quoting Troy.

"'Did you ever feel like there's this whole other person inside of you just looking for a way to come out?'" Nini offered. She appreciated Gabriella's line even more right now.

Seb stepped forward. "'Sharpay's kinda cute, too,'" he said.

The whole cast gave the response: "'So is a mountain lion, but you don't pet it!'"

Miss Jenn laughed and beamed proudly at the cast and crew. "And I'll just say, no matter what happens today, 'we're all in this together.' Okay, Wildcats, take a moment to settle your nerves. If we had a curtain, it would be up in twenty minutes!"

Nini glanced over at Ricky. She couldn't deny she had feelings for him, but was she just being the Gabriella to his Troy? Ricky caught Nini's eye and had similar feelings. Was this feeling, at this moment, part of the show or was it real?

The lights flashed in the hallway. Showtime!

Miss Jenn was handing out programs when she saw Ricky's dad. He came over to ask how his son was doing.

"I think he's gonna surprise you," she said.

"I've learned to stop being surprised by him," Mike said. He smiled at her. "I owe that to you."

Miss Jenn blushed, and she would have cherished the compliment if Ricky's mom hadn't walked up at that moment. They seemed to have come to the show together, and Miss Jenn backed out of the conversation quickly.

The show started and Ricky and Nini began their song, "Start of Something New." Miss Jenn found Mr. Mazzara in the back of the gym. "I need your engineering genius," she said.

Mr. Mazzara knew how to work the school gym tech console. He was willing to help, but he had a favor to ask, too. He wanted her to distribute robotics club stickers to the crowd and get some community interest.

"Done!" Miss Jenn exclaimed.

Down in the wings, Kourtney was freaking out about going on as Taylor. Nini gave her the prop Treo phone. "Trust the process," she said, quoting Miss Jenn.

Their first scenes went off well, as did Ricky and E.J.'s. Miss Jenn joined the cast backstage before the big "Stick to the Status Quo" number.

"How is the Taylor dance break going to work?" Seb asked. "Gina's tray-ography is really complex."

Carlos offered to tell the orchestra to cut that part, but Kourtney stood up. "Or we could just have Gina do it."

Gina was in the doorway holding a tray of cupcakes. "A friend bought me a last-minute flight back. I was gonna drop off these cupcakes and then hide in the gym and cheer you guys on."

Kourtney was not going to let Gina hide in the audience. "I was Taylor, and it was nice," she said. "But now it's your turn to save my butt for the dance." She held out the bedazzled tray. "Please, I'm asking you."

Gina turned to Miss Jenn. "Can I?" she asked.

"Of course," Miss Jenn told Gina. But she let Kourtney know she wasn't done with her yet. "You come see me after Christmas break," she told her.

Gina's number was a showstopper. She nailed the dance. The show continued on without a hitch and the crowd really seemed to be enjoying it.

Ricky saw Gina backstage and went over to her. "I still can't believe you're actually back," he said.

"Yeah." She grinned. "Don't blink or you'll miss me."

Ricky smiled. It was confusing seeing Gina. So much had happened in the week she was gone. "I don't know what to say," he said.

"It's time to 'get'cha head in the game,'" she told him. "Go fly, dude!"

Ricky put on his harness and was high above the audience when he spotted Todd, his mother's new boyfriend. The hope of his parents getting back together came crashing down. He lost his focus and felt a little out of sync with the dance, too. His head was definitely not in the game. He needed to talk to Nini, but she was out onstage.

"Nini seems a little nervous," Carlos said as he stood in the wings.

"Why? What happened?" Ricky asked.

Kourtney pointed out to the audience. "See that lady with the clipboard? That's the dean of that performing arts school she was looking at."

"You invited her?" Ricky asked. His face went white as he looked out into the audience at the dean and Todd. Suddenly, he really didn't feel well. Ricky found E.J. in the dressing room and threw him Troy's tank top. "You need to do the second act as Troy," he said.

E.J. was shocked. "Are you sick?" he asked.

"No, I'm good," Ricky said. "Good enough to help Nini get where she wants to go."

E.J. didn't really understand what Ricky was talking about.

"I'm screwing up out there," Ricky went on. "I can't blow this for Nini. There's someone in the audience who can change Nini's life, and she needs her best shot to impress him." He held out the shirt. "Will you do it?"

Taking the shirt, E.J. wasn't sure what to think. But he slid the tank on and was ready to play Troy.

CHAPTER 10

ACT TWO

Based on the episode
by Tim Federle

Just as act two was about to begin, Ashlyn spotted E.J. in the dressing room wearing Troy Bolton's basketball tank. "What did you do to Ricky?" she asked, panicked.

"I didn't do anything," E.J. told her. "He asked me to fill in."

"I guess a certain part of me wants to say congratulations," said Ashlyn. Then she had a thought. "Wait, if you're playing Troy, then who's playing Chad?"

Carlos walked in from the side stage, dressed in a super-baggy Wildcats tank. "Buckle up, Wildcats," he said awkwardly. He held up his hand to fist-bump E.J. "You ready, bro?"

He then turned to Ashlyn and looked at her pleadingly. "Pray for me!" he said in a slight panic.

Onstage, Nini looked out in the audience and saw the dean of Youth Actors Conservatory jotting down notes. Was she writing good things about her performance? Nini couldn't believe her dream of going to drama school might actually become a reality.

After their scene, Nini and Gina headed back to the dressing room, excited by how well it had gone. Nini admired Gina's confidence. She always seemed to be sure of herself and her performance.

"You've played a lot more leading roles than I have," Nini told her. "What do you do when there's someone in the audience who could change your life?"

"Nini, listen, you're a great actor," Gina said. "So just act like someone who knows what she's doing."

"Does that ever work?" Nini asked.

"Works for me everywhere I go," Gina said. "It's my greatest trick. Also sort of my only trick."

Nini gave Gina a hug. She was happy Gina had

come back for the show—and actually sad that she would be leaving again.

Outside in the hallway, Ricky was pacing. He texted Nini to tell her why he was bailing out on the show. He also sent a text to his parents.

On her cue, Nini walked back onstage. She was surprised to see E.J.—not Ricky. She covered her microphone. "Where's Ricky?" she asked. E.J. pushed on with the scene. Nini was so confused—and hurt.

Next Ashlyn sang her big number, with Big Red watching admiringly. Backstage, Nini sat with Kourtney in the dressing room wondering why Ricky would just leave in the middle of the show.

"You haven't heard from him?" Kourtney asked.

Nini went to get her phone and saw Ricky's text.

S.O.S., he wrote. *Don't freak out but E.J. is going on as Troy. I am so sorry. My mom's boyfriend showed up and I'm a mess. You deserve a real leading man in front of that scout.*

"Well, I guess that's sort of sweet . . . in a really dumb way," Kourtney said.

This was definitely not how Nini had pictured opening night.

Ricky's mom found her son in the hallway. She was worried about him. Was it just stage fright? "You've made a commitment to this," she told him. "People are counting on you."

"You're one to talk about commitment," Ricky mumbled. He glared at his mom. "It's not about nerves. It's about doing something for somebody I care about."

Knowing there was something else bothering Ricky, his mom pressed him. "What's going on?" she asked.

"Why did you bring him to the show?" Ricky blurted out. He still couldn't believe that his mom would bring her *boyfriend* to his show.

"Todd? I wanted him to meet you," she said. "I didn't want to say anything before the show because I didn't want to throw you off."

Ricky scoffed. While he was levitating above the audience was not the ideal time either! "How do you think Dad feels?" he asked.

"Honestly," she said, "I think Dad is happy that I'm happy."

"You two looked plenty happy before the show started," he said. "You were hugging. I saw it. It was like how it used to be."

Looking at Ricky, she gave a long exhale. "Ricky," she said, "not all couples are meant to be together."

Her words weighed heavily on Ricky. He heard the music start for "Bop to the Top" and left to go watch Seb perform.

Seb was in the wings and not going onstage on his cue. Carlos found him and gave him a pep talk about how he was the only one who could pull off this Sharpay role, but Seb wasn't nervous about going on as Sharpay. He was nervous about disappointing the three rows of his family members who had come out to support him. Carlos was a little envious of all that support. "Count your blessings," he told Seb.

"And dance your heart out! Bop to the sky, baby!"

Up in the tech console, Big Red and Mr. Mazzara were busy working the lighting board. Big Red's technical skills were not lost on his teacher. "Young man, have you considered applying to my robotics club?" he asked.

Big Red grinned. He knew he had found his talent—and he was enjoying every minute.

Gina found Ricky by the water fountain outside the gym. When he told her about his mom's boyfriend being in the audience, she asked if that was the only reason he gave up playing Troy.

"Honestly, this is Nini's big moment," he confessed. "The best thing I can do for her is just take a step back and . . . watch."

Gina wasn't sure that was true, but she wanted to support Ricky. She encouraged him to watch the show with her from the back of the gym. "Let's go watch E.J. Caswell sweep himself off his feet," she said.

Ricky laughed, despite how he was feeling. He was glad Gina was back. Nini saw the two of them come in from her spot on center stage. She froze and missed her line.

"Remember kindergarten?" E.J. said again. Only this time, he ad-libbed the next line. "There's nothing like the friends you made back then. And they never really leave, do they?"

Nini looked confused. She put her hand on her mike. "What are you doing?"

"Something right, I hope," E.J. replied, covering his mike. "I'm going to play to lose. I'm not the Troy you want." He backed away into the dark wings.

Nini knew what she had to do. She began singing "Breaking Free" and walked out of the spotlight into the audience toward Ricky. She held up her phone and hit the flashlight to shine on him.

"I'm really not at my best," Ricky said, unsure of what Nini wanted him to do.

"Look at me, Ricky," Nini said, quoting the movie. "Right at me."

She continued to sing. By the time she got to the chorus, the orchestra was playing. Ricky took her hand and joined Nini in the song. He could forget everything that had happened tonight when he was singing with Nini. Together, they headed to center stage. Their voices blended in perfect harmony, and their chemistry was amazing.

Gina watched them and smiled. They were a great couple, on and off the stage.

"Some wonderstudies we are, huh?" E.J. kidded, joining her at the back of the gym.

Gina smiled. "Yeah, we are," she told him. She turned to face him. "Thank you for buying me that plane ticket."

"It didn't seem fair for you to miss all of this," E.J. said.

The song ended, and Nini and Ricky soaked in all the applause.

"That . . . just happened," Nini said, gushing. They raced backstage to change into their finale outfits. Nini was finally going to get to wear that red dress onstage.

"We're All in This Together" began, and the cast went through their bows as the audience clapped and sang along. As Nini and Ricky were about to go back out onstage, Ricky leaned in. "Can I ask you a question?" he said.

"Can it wait until we bow?" Nini asked.

After their well-deserved curtain call, Nini and Gina left the stage. Gina dragged Miss Jenn out into the spotlight, and Nini came back holding a bedazzled lunch tray with a red apple. She looked over at Miss Jenn. "You know what to say," she said.

Miss Jenn clutched her heart. This was a dream come true! "Is that the last apple?" she asked. The crowd cheered, and starting chanting, "Wildcats, Wildcats. . . ." This was a big moment for Miss Jenn. She stood onstage soaking in the applause.

"This is kind of the best," Ricky said.

"Oh, honey, wait till you see what I picked for the spring musical," Miss Jenn told him.

Big Red had a surprise as well. Just as Mr. Mazzara thought publicizing his robotics program was not going to happen, Big Red hit a button that released thousands of robotics club stickers into the crowd like confetti. Mr. Mazzara grinned.

After the show, the cast returned backstage. They still didn't know who had sent the giant flower arrangement.

Carlos searched and found a card. He read the inscription: TO ASHLYN, BECAUSE YOU GET ME.

Ashlyn looked over at E.J. "E.J., really," she gushed.

"I didn't write that," E.J. said.

Big Red stepped forward. "I did."

Ashlyn's heart stopped. That was incredibly sweet of Big Red. As the room began to clear out, she thanked him for the massive arrangement. They both shared a smile and headed out to join the rest of the cast and their families in the hallway.

"Have you seen Nini?" Ricky asked Kourtney.

"She's packing up," she told him. "That boarding school person took off, and I think she's taking it pretty hard."

Ricky found Nini in the dressing room. "I'm sorry that teacher chick left," he said. "She doesn't know what she's missing."

"It's okay," Nini said. "Honestly, I was kind of dying to get in all of the sudden, but now she's gone, and it looks like I'm meant to be at East High."

She looked up at Ricky. "Wait," she said, "what was your question from before we bowed?"

"Oh, I was . . ." Ricky stalled. He took a deep breath. "I was just gonna say, what happens now? I never opened a show or closed one. So what happens now?"

"Usually the theater kids cry and we go to Denny's," she replied.

"I mean now that it's all . . . over," Ricky said, feeling the weight of his words.

Nini stared at him, wishing that he would say more. What was he feeling? She wasn't sure and felt awkward, so she grabbed her backpack to head out.

"Don't you and Big Red have like three months of video games to catch up on?" Nini asked.

"Yeah, I guess so," he said.

"Is that it?" Nini asked. She started to walk away.

"I love you," Ricky blurted out.

This stopped Nini in her tracks. She turned to him.

"I've loved you since the first time you picked up your ukulele and wrote a song about clouds," he said. "And that night in your room, when you told me you loved me, I meant to say it, and I've kicked myself every day since then because I didn't say it. But I do. I love you."

Ricky went on to recall a time in seventh grade when they'd gone on a roller coaster and he puked on her shoes. She had been so cool about it and just shrugged the whole thing off by saying that she had wanted to get rid of the shoes because she had outgrown them. "But the thing is," Ricky told her. "I never outgrew you." Nini's eyes welled up. "I don't know what happens tomorrow, but I want this feeling to keep going. I'm not ready for it to be over. For us to be over. And if that means doing another musical, fine."

Nini laughed. "I get to pick the musical," she said.

"Fine," Ricky said, smiling. "I don't want this to just be a show-mance. I want it to be the real thing. I think it is the real thing. I want a chance to prove it."

Nini put her hand on Ricky's arm. "You know how in musicals, people burst into song when they've run out of things to say?"

Ricky nodded.

"Sometimes," Nini said, moving closer, "it's easier to just kiss."

The kiss was perfect. They exchanged opening night gifts. Nini gave Ricky dog tags engraved with TO FREAKY CALLBACK BOY, and Ricky gave Nini a gold guitar pick engraved with TO FREAKY MATH GIRL.

There was a knock on the door, and Kourtney stuck her head in. Nini's moms and grandmother were eager for her to come out for pictures and hugs. Nini left Ricky to pack up his things.

Out in the hallway, the cast and crew were getting ready to head to Ashlyn's house for an opening night celebration.

"Hey, are you coming?" Ashlyn asked Gina.

"I'm flying back in a couple of hours," Gina said.

"Cancel it," Ashlyn said. "You can spend the night in our guest room. Honestly, you can stay through Christmas if you want. Or actually . . ." Suddenly Ashlyn had a great idea, and by the look on Gina's face, she was thinking the same thing.

Principal Gutierrez interrupted Miss Jenn and Mr. Mazzara in mid-conversation. He informed them that they were the ones who had started the fire in the theater. Miss Jenn and Mr. Mazzara were shocked into speechlessness.

In the lobby, people were still mingling as the cast made their way to the front of the school. Nini didn't expect to see the dean of Youth Actors Conservatory standing there as well. She hadn't left the show. She had just stepped out to make a phone call . . . to the president of the board!

"Nini, you have talent, but more than that, you have a unique voice," the dean told her. "It's clear you have things to say. I'd like to offer you a spot starting next month." She handed Nini her card. "You'll let me know."

Nini stood silent for a moment as the lobby cleared out. Ricky peeked his head back in the door. "Hey, Nini! Ready to go?" he asked. This was the most incredible opening night ever. But she had to wonder, were all her dreams coming true? Was this truly the start of something new?